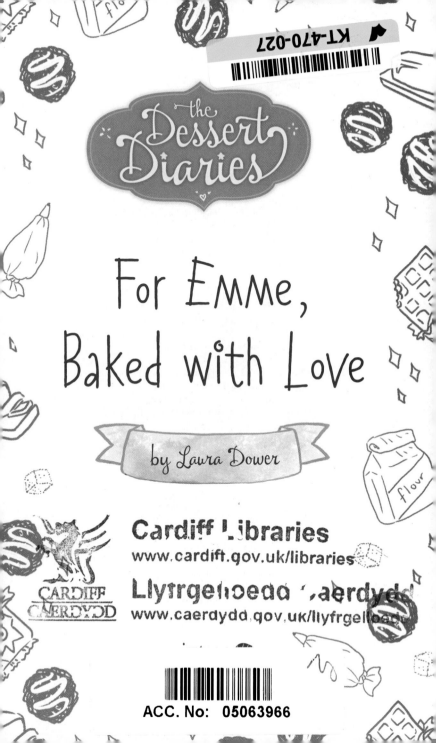

the Dessert Diaries

For Emme, Baked with Love

by Laura Dower

Raintree is an imprint of Capstone Global Library Limited, a company incorporated in England and Wales having its registered office at 264 Banbury Road, Oxford, OX2 7DY – Registered company number: 6695582

www.raintree.co.uk
myorders@raintree.co.uk

Edited by Kristen Mohn
Designed by Philippa Jenkins
Original illustrations © 2017 Capstone Global Limited Library
Illustrated by Lilly Lazuli
Production by Kathy McColley
Originated by Capstone Global Limited Library
Printed and bound in China.

ISBN 978 1 4747 2216 2
20 19 18 17 16
10 9 8 7 6 5 4 3 2 1

British Library Cataloguing in Publication Data
A full catalogue record for this book is available from the British Library.

Contents

The Grand Opening

Hello, Sweeties!

You may have noticed a few new neighbours with oven gloves moving in around this area. That's me and my baking posse!!! Get to know us better by clicking on "Meet the bakers". Better yet, come by and say hello at our Grand Opening on **12 October**! We've moved into the absolutely gorgeous building at the end of the High Street, the quaint brick one with the number 1899 carved in stone.

So, who are we? Well, we call ourselves **Daisy's Desserts**. At first I thought I should call our bakery Just Desserts, but that was taken. Then I considered some even worse ideas ...

Crumby (not so positive)
A Token of My Confection (too wordy)
Best Bakery Ever (boring!)
Lost In Frosting (huh?!)

So the naming was tough, but the decision to open was easy! I love this bakery as if it were my own child.

True story: My Nana Belle was the original baker in my family. She gave my sisters and me a love of all things sweet and baked. And bread! She could bake loaves of the most wonderful, warm bread that was perfect squish on the inside and crusty crisp on the outside. Is there anything better? Unless you're gluten free, of course. But I have learned to be a friendly baker for *all* my friends — we cater to your special needs!

In fact, I think I know exactly what kind of cake I am going to bake for you.

Come and find out!

Daisy Duncan (at your service!)

Chapter 1

Sweet dream come true

It was a Thursday morning, a cool, blue-sky kind of ordinary morning, and Emme stood across the street from the old brick building with the raggedy, spotted awning. Her thick black hair glistened in the sun. Emme tugged on her oversized jumper and readjusted the enormous flowered backpack on her back. What was going on over there? Emme squinted from under her brand-new, make-me-look-really-clever, tortoiseshell-framed glasses at the painted wooden sign that had been placed out the front:

Dive into Daisy's Desserts, OPENING SOON

A bakery? This was a dream come true! A *sweet*

dream. This corner shop had been many things over the years: a café that only served noodles, a fancy boutique most people couldn't afford, a dusty comic book shop, a hardware shop, and a load of other things Mum and Dad had told Emme they remembered from when *they* were small. (They'd both grown up in this neighbourhood too – *child-hood sweethearts*! Her mum's parents owned a Japanese restaurant, and her dad's first job was as their waiter. Kamiko and Charlie had been together ever since – actually, since they were just a few years older than Emme's age now. Weird!)

But if there was one thing in the entire universe that *did* make sense, it was dessert. Yes, Emme had her best friends Lizzie and Trish, but Emme's first love was sweet stuff: cookies, sweets and all things sugary. In the mixed-up, crazy universe of Emme Remmers, dessert was a bona fide food group.

She had to get a closer look at that bakery. Looking both ways, Emme ran across the street towards the shop. She pressed her nose to the window and peered inside through an enormous rip in the brown paper that covered it. Were people in there? Was that music playing? Emme felt a deep drumbeat through the glass. Inside was a whole world of vintage posters, antique display cases, and little pink and white lights strung all over. Someone had transformed this boring old hardware shop seemingly overnight.

Through the rip in the paper, Emme spied round and square wooden tables already set up for customers, each one decorated with a different, brightly coloured tablecloth. An enormous chalkboard had been hung behind one of the glass cases on a side wall. Painted at the top was: *Try One (Or Two)!* Below this was a wide, blank space that Emme guessed was for the daily list of baked goods. Her tummy rumbled loudly at the notion of all that wonderful butter and sugar and glazed everything that would soon be for sale. She could spend an entire year's pocket money here, no problem.

All at once, the door to the bakery burst open with a loud squeak. A rush of warm air swirled around Emme like a hug.

Mmmmmm. Warm cookie smell. Nothing better.

A man flew out with boxes in his arms. "Whoa!" he yelped, balancing the boxes on his wide hip while he fished in his pocket. "Didn't see you there, kiddo."

In that moment Emme could smell the cookies and so many more things coming from inside: caramel and strawberry and roasted almonds ... and chocolate! And now energetic music poured out of the bakery door too, in a river of sound. The notes lifted up and out onto the street – twangy guitars and bass drums. Someone inside was wailing along with the song. For a brief moment, she felt like the bakery was literally calling out to her in every way that it could, begging her to come and see, listen and especially taste.

"You like cake?" the man asked. His apron, which was covered with stains and flour, had the name Carlos printed on the front. There was even flour dusting his salt and pepper tuft of hair.

"Who doesn't like cake?" Emme answered with a meek shrug.

"Well, Daisy always says people don't eat enough cake. We open tomorrow, officially, by the way," Carlos said, grinning. "Whatever you do, don't miss the apple bars. Daisy's food is pure magic, baked love."

"What's baked love?" Emme giggled.

"You'll know when you taste it," Carlos said and laughed. "And when you meet Daisy."

"It's like this place just appeared overnight," Emme said. "Last time I looked, there were saws and hammers on display."

"Magic everywhere!" Carlos said, winking. "We'd been planning for a long time and then Daisy found this perfect location available, right here in the middle of everything. Now we're installing ovens, tables, cabinets. It's going to be a special spot," Carlos said. He headed off down the street, boxes perched high on his shoulder. "Come to the opening tomorrow!" he called back.

Emme's stomach rumbled again at the idea of magic cake. Who could resist something called *baked love*? Not Emme. She could use some extra love at the moment. Things at home had been a little tense.

When she peered inside the shop again, Emme's eyes fell upon an enormous clock mounted to the wall. It was as large as a window. The clock read eight-thirty. Oh, no! How had it got so late? Emme was going to miss the first bell at school.

She slung her bag back over her shoulder and speed-walked the rest of the way to school. Luckily, a handful of other pupils were just making it up the steps in time for the second bell like she was.

Emme slipped quietly into her seat in the hall, unnoticed. Each morning all the classes gathered in the assembly room and waited for the teachers to come and collect their pupils. But once a week there was a school meeting, so pupils could count on the teachers being a little late those days. Lucky for Emme, today's meeting seemed to be running extra long. She could daydream for a little bit – and she wouldn't even get a late slip.

"I'm so glad you're here *finally*!" Lizzie said, sneaking into the seat next to Emme. She flipped her blond, curly bob. "Did you finish the English homework? Because I didn't understand *anything,* and I swear that maths test next week is going to be impossible, don't you think?"

"I guess," Emme mumbled, her mind in a cloud of sugar and chocolate icing.

Lizzie leaned in and cocked her head. "I swear, sometimes I think I could just die, we get so much homework. Emme? Are you even listening?"

Emme was *always* listening, of course. How could she not? Because Lizzie was *always* talking. Lizzie, with her perfect purple top and harem pants.

"Do you like apple bars?" Emme asked.

"Apple – what?" Lizzie frowned. "What are you

talking about? See? I knew you weren't listening."

"Incoming!" a very upbeat Trish, decked out in bright green tracksuit bottoms and an orange hoodie, came over and squeezed into a seat near the pair. "OMG that homework was so hard, right? I had volleyball last night, and I waited until after practice to do it. I thought it was going to be easy. NOT!"

Trish was Emme's other best friend at school. She had long auburn brown plaits with rainbow beads that clicked and clacked every time she tossed her head. As one of the top volleyball players on the school team, Trish always made a racket when she spiked the ball. She loved sport as much as Emme loved dessert.

"Do *you* like apple bars?" Emme asked Trish.

"What's with the apple bars? Seriously, Ems?" Lizzie asked, making a funny face.

Trish just laughed. "Actually," she said, "I love apple bars. Do you have one? I'm still hungry even though I ate two breakfasts."

The loudspeaker boomed, and somebody announced that the school meeting was running long – "Obviously!" Lizzie said – so the teachers would not be down for ten more minutes. The girls pulled out their homework to compare notes. Emme plucked her English notebook from her backpack and showed the girls her answers.

"You knew what to put for number six?" Lizzie asked. "Ugh, I'm so jelly roll."

"Jelly roll?" Emme asked and thought again of Daisy's Desserts.

"You know, like *jealous,*" Trish said and high-fived Lizzie. "And I'm a bit jelly too. You are so much cleverer than us, Ems. It must be so easy being you."

"Definitely," Lizzie said, sighing.

Emme shrugged, like always. "Not really, but thanks, I think?"

Emme wished she could do more than just shrug, but she wasn't feeling anything more than *meh*. Lizzie and Trish knew *something* was up, but Emme wasn't saying much lately. She wasn't doing much either besides her homework and staying in her bedroom playing Blox on her smartphone or reading another Inspector Morgan book. This was a big change from how Emme usually acted. Emme used to be the one who planned crazy activities for the three of them, like beach day in January, or dressing backwards for school-spirit day. Emme was the one who always texted the funniest cat memes or suggested they sell candy floss instead of cookies for a school sale.

But lately Emme had been changing plans at the last minute. Twice, she forgot that she was supposed to meet Trish at the library. And she decided not to try out for the football team even though the three friends had agreed they'd all do it together. Lizzie and Trish knew something was wrong, but they didn't know how to ask Emme what it was.

Emme hadn't told anyone the full truth about how much her mum and dad had been fighting over the past few months. It was always some version of the same thing: Work was hard for mum, work was harder for dad, mum was lonely, dad was stressed, the flat was a mess, they wanted to move, they didn't want to move and a load of other seemingly disconnected things that somehow all added up to ARGUMENTS. Emme's role as only child was to keep the peace, but that was getting harder to do. Whenever a fight would rumble after dinner or at bedtime, Emme had become an expert at disappearing behind her painted sky-blue bedroom door.

Her parents' marriage hadn't always felt rocky. But things shifted a while ago, when Dad began to travel more for his job at a computer software company. Mum was working a lot too, as a teacher in the local nursery school. Now, more than ever, there was conflict – at every meal, every outing and every goodnight. Mum was the yeller. Dad was the crier. Talk about uncomfortable! Dad would get all shaky and upset whenever mum began barking at him.

Why couldn't they just stop making each other so miserable? They didn't seem to know how. It's like they forgot how to love each other. Now they were about to celebrate their thirteenth wedding anniversary, though "celebrate" didn't seem like the right word.

Emme had already begun planning a way to surprise her parents with a very special gift for their anniversary. Every year she planned some surprise, and every year she tried to outdo whatever she had come up with the year before. This year she was going to find something that would make them feel more loved – and more *loving*. She was going to give them the perfect gift. The only problem was, what would the perfect gift be?

The school day felt like a slow-moving mud slide. Emme had trouble concentrating, and for some reason her thoughts kept drifting back to the bakery. Baked love sounded nice, whatever that was.

"Hey, a new bakery is opening down the street from my flat," Emme said to Lizzie and Trish at lunch. She told them about the Grand Opening festivities. "Wanna go?" she asked.

"We should totally go after school tomorrow," Lizzie suggested. "I am, after all, the original party animal."

"And I will never turn my back on a free sample," Trish added.

This cheered up Emme enormously, especially since she had spent so little time with her friends outside of school lately. They agreed that they would go to the bakery opening and munch through all of the tasty treats to get their weekend off to a good start.

Maybe they'd just stay in the new bakery forever, talking and laughing and staking out one of those little wooden tables as their very own, so that Emme wouldn't have to go home to her bickering parents.

Chapter 2

Belly up to the apple bar

"I can't believe I actually thought about what outfit I'd wear for this bakery opening," Emme said, giggling to her friends. "That's one for the lame hall of fame."

"Not lame! Totally *cute*," said Lizzie. "I love your yellow dotted socks too. Dots are *waaay* in."

Emme had selected those socks on purpose. She also wore a denim shirt tied at the waist over a yellow vest over dark blue jeans. Glitter blue Converse trainers completed the look along with the polka-dot socks.

"You are always so matchy-matchy," Trish said. "But in a good way, I suppose." She nudged Emme playfully.

"And you're so random! In a *good way*, I suppose," Emme teased back. Trish had on a pair of purple-and-white checked trousers and an oversized brown sweatshirt with a bear face on it. Trish never matched *anything*. She had, without question, hands down, one-hundred per cent, THE most random wardrobe of anyone in Year 7.

"Random is always good," Trish replied. "Especially on the football pitch. It keeps the opponent guessing!"

The girls laughed. No one in their trio seemed to mind too much what other people thought about their unique fashion choices. Life was bigger than an expensive shirt from Zone Department Store or some other too-cool label, wasn't it?

As they approached the Grand Opening event Friday after school, talk of their outfits stopped and they stared in awe at the hubbub. The street was mobbed, elbow-to-elbow with people waiting to get into Daisy's Desserts. This was not at all what Emme had expected. She had thought there might be a short queue to the door and some people politely tasting a cookie or two. She had no idea there would be utter and complete chaos.

"Stay in the queue, please," a voice bellowed through a bullhorn. "Come on people!"

What *was* this craziness? Police had placed orange sawhorse barriers to keep people from parking near the shop entrance. A group of officers stood at the corner, probably on the lookout for people getting trampled or body surfing on the large crowd. It seemed that *everyone* within a one-kilometre radius of Daisy's Desserts had come to have a look at the place.

The closer the queue drew to the bakery's entrance, the more excited the crowd became. People always say some moments are "electric", and now Emme was realizing what they meant.

TV news reporter (and local celebrity) Dave Yu was on the scene to do a live broadcast. Dave did local interest reports and restaurant reviews. This was a combination of both.

"Greetings from Daisy's Desserts!" he boomed into his mic.

"Dave Yu!" Lizzie exclaimed. "Let's go and stand behind him and get on TV!"

Emme rolled her eyes. The last thing on her mind was a TV debut. "Do we really need to be on television? We're just here to get some sugar," she pleaded.

Lizzie grinned. "Fifteen minutes of fame, Em."

"Does my hair look okay?" Emme asked, suddenly worried about the camera.

"Ha! It's all sticking up with static," Trish said.

Emme giggled. Maybe there really was electricity in the air!

"No fame is worth this wait. This queue is going to take forever," Trish complained. But almost as if by magic, as soon as Trish said that, the queue began to move. Between the police and the bakery staff, the crowd kept moving in synch.

"Maybe we should have come on a less busy day," Lizzie said. They felt crushed by the mob of people eagerly seeking yummy free samples from Daisy's Desserts. The whole place was buzzing – and glowing too, from the metallic streamers and shimmery lights that had been strung up outside the bakery. Tables were set up on the pavement. A large coffee cart made cappuccinos to order. As the girls edged towards the entrance, they heard a chorus of "*mmmmms*" and "*aahhhhs*" from visitors carrying out mini-plates of tasty bites. Emme noticed that *their* hair was sort of sticking up too! This was the grandest opening the girls had ever witnessed, and Emme was delighted to be right in the middle of it all.

Carlos had been right about the baked love. Everything outside *and* inside Daisy's Desserts seemed enchanted. And then there was that news crew! Maybe it wouldn't be so bad to have a starring role in tonight's six o'clock news?

"Okay, let's get on the news," Emme said mischievously, as if she'd been possessed by some kind of sudden confidence. Maybe her old fun-loving spark was returning. Was it bakery brav-ery? Emme tried to smooth down her electric hair so she wouldn't look totally nuts. As the cameraman panned the crowd, the girls leaped into the air to be noticed.

Dave Yu turned to the crowd. "All this for an apple bar?" he asked the crowd. Everyone cheered. One tattooed guy kneeled next to his girlfriend and proposed on camera. The girls dropped their jaws and then applauded when his tattooed girlfriend said, "Yes!"

"Look!" Lizzie cried. "Wave! We're on camera!"

Emme and Trish waved shyly while Lizzie yelled, "Hi, Mum!" into the camera.

When they finally stepped inside the actual bak-ery, it was clear to Emme that there was definitely something unusual about it. *In a good way*, as Trish would say. But Emme couldn't quite put her finger on it.

The brown paper that had been hanging inside the oversized glass windows was gone. Painted on the gleaming shop windows were the words *DAISY'S DESSERTS. Try One (Or Two)!* Daisy and her team had hung golden gingham curtains at the corners of the windows, which gave the whole place a homey feeling. Inside, the furniture was cozily mismatched, with different coloured and sized wooden chairs pulled up to the many random wooden tables. Anti-matching. Trish *loved* that detail when she saw it.

All of the walls had been painted with creamy pale tones, like icing. A large metal coffee cup hung behind the old-fashioned brass cash register along with a large tin sign that read *EAT MORE CAKE*. It was exactly what Carlos had said – Daisy's orders. And assorted painted wooden daisies were hung up on the wall too, for obvious reasons.

The oversized wooden counter and glass case at the back of the bakery was now overflowing with cakes and cookies in all shapes and sizes.

"This is insane! I love it!" Lizzie cried.

"Me too," Trish said. "I want to try one of everything."

"Clearly so does everyone else!" Emme giggled.

"Well, hello, girls!" came a voice from behind them. A tall woman with frizzy red hair edged past the threesome. "Welcome! Welcome!" she called behind her with a smile.

"Did you see that? Her apron said 'DAISY,'" Lizzie said excitedly. "I wonder if that's HER."

"Of course it's her!" Emme said cheerfully, thinking that this was exactly how she had imagined the mysterious Daisy would look.

The three girls turned their attention to Daisy, now standing inside the shop, welcoming her customers. Emme wondered if maybe, just maybe, the magic Daisy brought to this place was *actual* magic. Did she cast spells on her flour and sugar and butter so it tasted even better than usual? How exactly did she *bake* love?

A family stood up to leave, and Emme managed to grab their empty table. She swooped in and shoved her backpack on top, nearly knocking over a glass sugar shaker.

"Careful!" another woman from the shop cried out. She came over as Lizzie and Trish took a seat. She had brown skin, a long grey plait, cat's-eye glasses and an apron straining over her chest that read 'DINA'. "Watch the nuts," Dina cracked. "And I'm not talking about the brownies!"

The girls laughed. Dina was, of course, talking about the customers – probably including Emme and her friends. The surging crowd continued.

"Of course we knew it'd be busy, but my! This place is bopping," Dina said. "I'm tired already. Where are you girls from?"

"We go to school not far from here," Emme said. "And I live right down the street."

"Well, then, you'll be regulars, won't you!" Dina declared. "Whatcha want to nosh?"

"Carlos told me your apple bars are the best. I ran into him yesterday. He works here too, right?" Emme asked.

Dina laughed. "Works here is an understatement! He's the engine for this whole machine.

Daisy's Desserts would be a dud without him. And yes, the apple bars are everyone's favourite. Go and try! There's a brand-new batch – fresh out of the oven. Belly up to the apple bar!"

"We will!" Emme said.

"We'll belly up to everything!" Trish added.

"Head over to the sample station. If you're lucky, you'll have a chance to try one of the truffle tarts too. Made 'em myself. The samples are flying off the table!"

"What's a truffle tart?" Lizzie made a face. "Sounds like something funky I *don't* want to eat."

"A truffle is a special treat made of chocolate, butter, cream, sugar, and dusted with cocoa powder," Dina said. "And Daisy adds her own special ingredient ... oh, I shouldn't say anything."

Lizzie hopped up. "Chocolate? I take it back. I want *all* the truffle tarts. Let's go!"

"You two go first. I'll save our table," Emme said, enjoying the scene.

Trish and Lizzie rushed off to the sample table.

"You and your pals having fun?" Frizzy-haired Daisy appeared out of nowhere and stood at Emme's small table in the corner, offering a tray with cream puffs on it. She handed a small plate to Emme, who happily sampled a miniature pink cookie.

"The rose snaps are delish ... and you've got to try the whipped cream puff," Daisy said, raising an eyebrow towards the larger tray.

"*Mmmm,*" Emme said, taking a mouthful. "*Mmmmm ... fffffun.*"

"Ha!" Daisy said, chuckling. "Now that's the sound of baked goods!"

She turned and was about to walk over to another cluster of customers when she stopped quite suddenly and walked back towards Emme with a curious look in her eyes.

"Here," Daisy said, digging in the pocket of her apron with her free hand. She gave Emme a handful of tiny flyers for the bakery with a web address and a quote: *A little sugar and cream is like a dream.*

"You look like someone who could help me out.

Tell your family and friends about this place, will you?" Daisy said. "Hope we see you and your friends here again, fingers and toes crossed. Any time you need a batch of baked love, you come on over, okay?"

"Oh, yes! Of course we will come back." Emme took the flyers and promised to spread the word.

Just then, Lizzie and Trish returned with their samples. They'd got a small plate for Emme too.

"Thanks so much!" Emme said. "Yum! I was just talking to Daisy about– "

"You were talking to Daisy? The *owner*?" Lizzie interrupted, looking around to catch a glimpse of the bakery's namesake.

"She stopped to ask me how we liked the place," Emme said, somewhat proudly.

"So much free food! This place is off-the-charts cool, Emme," Trish said. "I am so glad we came today – and that we waited in that way-too-long queue and everything."

"When we went to get our samples, we stood over by that sideboard and some woman – I am not kidding – started tap dancing," Lizzie said and put up jazz hands to demonstrate.

"I heard another little boy say that Daisy's cupcakes gave him superpowers, and then he made some lightning bolt move," Trish added with a laugh.

"What's going on around here?" Emme asked. There was definitely some sort of spell at work.

Lizzie primped a little and looked around. "I just wish we'd got on the news with that reporter."

Emme loved the idea of being in the middle of something this grand, like a caramel filling in the best chocolate sludge cake ever. It was so ooey-gooey alive in here.

"Hey, so what is up with that new boy in our class?" Lizzie asked Trish, changing the subject abruptly. "Does he live in your block of flats?"

"Yeah, why?" Trish said eyeing Lizzie sideways and licking icing sugar from her fingertips.

"What about him?" Emme asked curiously.

"So … do you like him?" Lizzie asked.

"Ooh, let's hear it!" Emme said, spraying truffle tart crumbs across the table in her excitement.

"Stop!" Trish said and practically choked on a chocolate chip. "Okay. Yes, there's a new boy at school – he started last month. He's in my block, so I see him in the lift all the time. And I stupidly mentioned him to Lizzie, but that's all. Kaput. End of story. Thanks a lot, Lizzie. You stink."

"The truth will set you free," Lizzie smirked, humming.

"You really like causing trouble, don't you?" Trish said, chucking a napkin at Lizzie.

"Yep," Lizzie admitted. "I like causing trouble."

Emme laughed out loud and tried to make light of the situation – and to change the subject. "Know what I like? More samples. Who's with me?"

"Me!" Trish said, getting up. "Your turn to watch the table, Lizzie."

"Fine. But get me one of those cake pops!"

Emme and Trish went back to the sample bar.

"Ugh," Trish said as the two moved through

the crowd. "I hate the fact that Lizzie always blabs about everything. You can't tell her *anything.*"

"Oh, it's not a big deal, is it? It's not like she said it in front of anyone but me," Emme said, trying to keep the peace. She was used to doing that, or trying to anyway.

"Not this time, but she will. It's just so embarrassing when she brings up stuff like that," Trish said. "She does that to me on Instagram too – posts stuff that's really not for everyone to see. It makes me not want to tell her *anything* personal."

"Yeah," Emme nodded. She had to admit Trish was right. Emme had confided in Lizzie back when her parents' fights first began. Then, a few weeks later, Lizzie had posted something on Instagram about her uncle and aunt splitting up and wrote, "You know what I mean, Em?" alerting the world that Emme *did* know about such things.

Emme and Trish agreed: better to keep the details of their lives under lock and key when it came to Lizzie. They didn't want their private business broadcast all over the place.

As a rule, just about the only thing Emme ever posted online was about her tropical fish tank. There wasn't much anyone could gossip about *that*.

Emme spotted the apple bar display and grabbed Trish by the wrist. "There they are! Yum!"

A plump, silver-haired woman was standing behind the case with the apple bars and a lot of other bars too: lemon, cranberry and even white chocolate chip. "Well, hello, ladies," the woman said with a wide smile. "I'm Babs. Want something wonderful?"

Babs had wrinkles on her wrinkles but her blue eyes glistened. She'd obviously been baking for a long, long time.

"What's your favourite treat so far?" she asked.

At the same time Trish and Emme said, "Truffle tarts," and then giggled.

Babs leaned in and whispered, "Mine too. That's from a recipe passed down by our owner Daisy's grandmother, Nana Belle. Nana Belle's the heart and soul of most of the recipes in this place – and she was my best friend, about a million years ago."

"She was?" Emme asked, surprised. "A million years ago?"

Babs winked and adjusted her beehive hairdo. "Yeah, well. A lotta years. We're all connected. We're all ingredients baked into one perfect pie."

Then Babs glanced down the counter to attend to another customer. A mum and her five sons were looking at the cherry cake pops. The boys were fighting, pulling hair, poking shoulders and causing general mayhem. But in a blink, when the cake pops touched their lips, they boys stopped horsing around and stood quietly, eating and smiling.

The mother looked astounded by the change. "I was just standing here wishing they would settle down and ... they did! Incredible." She shook her head in disbelief.

"We're at your service," Babs said with a knowing smile.

Trish gave Emme a look. "There is something seriously bizarre about this place!" she whispered.

"I was just thinking the same thing," Emme agreed. Was this some sort of wish-granting bakery?

Between Dina, Babs, Carlos and Daisy with her gravity-defying hair, the swarm of people with their dance routines and marriage proposals, the Dave Yu factor and that crazy electric hum, this place was going down in the Emme Remmers history book as the most one-of-a-kind place ever. Strange encounters made the place all the more perfect. So perfect that Emme never wanted to leave Daisy's Desserts.

As they walked back to the table, Lizzie made a face. "What took you so long?"

By now the girls were ready to explode from a pastry overload. They looked at the samples they had just brought back and realized they had over-done it.

"We should go," Trish said. "But I just need to sit

for one minute more. My tummy is hurting a little bit ..."

"We've also hogged this table for long enough," Emme said, looking around at the crowd that never seemed to end.

Babs came by while they were sitting, armed with three "demitasse" (aka teeny) cups of "sample" cocoa. She didn't seem to mind how long the girls stayed.

"*Bon appétit*, ladies! Stay as long as you like. Once you're here it's hard to leave ... that's Daisy's spell," Babs said with a tinkly laugh.

"*Merci*!" Emme said.

"*Beaucoup*!" Lizzie finished, and the three girls broke into a chorus of giggles, overwhelmed by sugar and the electric buzz they had felt from the moment they walked through the door.

Chapter 3

Sugar rush

When Emme burst into their flat, she still felt a little woozy from her Daisy-fuelled sugar rush. But she couldn't wait to tell her parents about the bakery Grand Opening and all of the wonderful people they'd met there. She dumped her backpack and headed for the kitchen.

In a moment of the most-perfect timing *ever*, the tiny kitchen TV was playing the local news. Just as Emme walked in, a short feature came on about "Crazy Daisy's!" That's what reporters were calling the chaos at the bakery opening, like nothing they'd ever seen before.

And who was on camera, front and centre in the middle of the bakery crowd?

Emme, Lizzie and Trish, of course!

"Mum!" Emme pointed to the TV. "Look! Look!"

"What?" Mum looked stunned. "Emme, that's you? Is *that* the new bakery you were talking about? My goodness! Wasn't that just a hardware shop? Oh, look at you three. How *sweet*!"

"*Mummm*," Emme made a face at Mum's lame pun.

Mum giggled. "It's your fifteen minutes of fame!"

"That's what Lizzie said! But it was more like fifteen seconds," Emme said. "You can hardly see us behind those other screaming people. But Daisy's is absolutely the best bakery I have ever visited in my entire short life. Seriously."

"Did you bring anything home for your sweet mother?" Mum said, raising one eyebrow.

Emme bit her lip. She thought of all she'd pigged out on and yet hadn't brought so much as a crumb home for Mum and Dad. Oops.

"Oh, um ... uh," Emme stammered. "I'm *sooooo* sorry, Mum. Well, there was so much going on and I– "

"Don't worry, I'm just teasing," Mum laughed. "We'll pick up cookies later."

"Maybe we can all walk down there with Dad?" Emme asked hopefully. "Like a family outing maybe?"

Mum rolled her eyes. "Well, that's unlikely. Your father is working late again. He has to leave on some trip this week too. It's a wonder he ever comes home for dinner anymore, is it? I suppose I could ask him, but you know how it is."

"Oh," Emme said softly. Mum was starting again. She complained about Dad all the time lately.

"I know I should be getting used to this," Mum went on. "But it seems like every day there is some kind of new trip or meeting on the schedule ..."

Her voice trailed off for a moment, and Emme didn't want to say anything that might lead to Mum getting even angrier about Dad or the situation.

So Emme kept her mouth shut.

But Mum kept on talking.

"Dad will have to watch the repeat of this news story online, I suppose," she said. "Not that he has time for that either since he's always finding some excuse to– "

"Mum! Stop!"

Mum looked at Emme, surprised by her outburst.

"Just stop," Emme repeated. Then she raced to her bedroom so she didn't have to hear the end of Mum's train of thought. She didn't want her mum to sour a day that had been so wonderfully baked and iced. She wanted to hold on to that perfect, sweet feeling.

Thankfully, Emme's bedroom was the ultimate refuge. The walls were a deep sea blue and on half of Emme's large work desk sat an enormous aquarium filled with dozens of fish in all colours. Emme loved everything about the sea. Her carpet looked like a river. Her wall was decorated with posters of dolphins and whales. Some people would have said that these were things Emme should have outgrown by Year 7. But she loved them all more than ever. One day, Emme dreamed of becoming an oceanographer. Once she'd seen a report about how the world's oceans had been overfished and overburdened with rubbish. So she dreamed about rescuing marine life and diving deep and saving the oceans one coral reef at a time.

Emme must have drifted off into a deep-sea sleep because she was awoken by a sharp knock on the bedroom door. Her room was completely dark now. More than an hour must have passed.

Knockity-knock.

"Go away, Mum, please," Emme said. "I just don't want to talk. I think I may just go to bed without any– "

"Em, it's Dad."

"Dad!"

Emme hopped out of her cushy blue beanbag chair as Dad turned the knob and poked his head inside. She smiled broadly as he came in. His tie was loosened and his suit jacket was off. He looked flushed, like he'd just run up the ten flights to their flat.

"How was work?" Emme asked. "Are you feeling okay? You look sort of, well, sweaty."

"Yeah, I should shower," Dad chuckled, jokingly sniffing his armpits.

Emme made a face. "Dad! That's disgusting."

"Come on, I'll clean up, and we'll go out to dinner," Dad said.

"All of us?" Emme asked as she twisted a piece of her long hair between her fingers.

Dad paused. "Yeah, all of us," he said. "I didn't think I would be home. But my meeting finished early tonight. And, hey, Mum told me that you were featured on some special news report. So you're famous, huh?"

Dad planted a sweaty kiss on her forehead.

"Hey, don't get sweat on the celebrity!" Emme teased, wiping it off.

Ten minutes later the three Remmers were headed towards a little pub called Dresner's not far from their flat. Emme always ordered their Salisbury steak dinner special. It sounded kind of gross at first but after one bite (loaded with ketchup of course), Emme was addicted. She always polished off her meal, in addition to half a bread basket.

Dinner conversation was *slooooooow*. The most anyone had said so far was, "Pass the salt." Dad was on his mobile phone most of the time, scrolling through messages for the things he'd probably left behind at the office. Mum poked at her food but didn't really eat much. Emme noticed these things – the way Mum and Dad pushed their chairs a little bit farther apart than usual, the way they didn't really make eye contact.

They were doing this dinner for her benefit, as they'd done so many times over the past months. Emme could tell when they were trying too hard, and she felt a bit guilty about the fact that they had to fake it. But on the other hand, she liked knowing that they were willing to try for her. Eventually, they'd get over this whole not-talking-to-each-other thing. They'd find a way to work it out. She hoped.

"Tell Dad about the news reporter," Mum said brightly. "I'm sure he wants to hear all about the bakery. Don't leave anything out."

Emme swallowed her bite of salad and said, "Well, there's this new bakery a few streets away, and we went there after school. A TV news reporter was there, and it was totally crazy." She rambled on about Daisy and all the free samples and the tattooed couple who were now engaged.

Dad nodded as he listened and laughed as Emme gave her best Dave Yu impression. "Impressive!"

"Emme looked so lovely on camera," Mum said. "So grown up!"

"Who gave you permission to grow up?" Dad joked.

"Come on, you two," Emme said. "How to be embarrassing. I looked okay – it was all about the outfit. There were so many people there. I was only on camera for, like, a second."

"Let's go and see the bakery," Dad said as he flipped his credit card onto the table to pay for dinner. "I want to see where this all happened – and taste some of those goodies."

"Now?" Emme cheered up. "Really? You'll love it!"

"Now?" Mum repeated doubtfully, looking at her watch.

They shuffled out of Dresner's in single file, Mum's hand on Emme's back, Dad bringing up the rear. Emme felt a twist of happy inside. This was an unusually good sign. Maybe Dad was trying to be more involved. Maybe Mum was trying not to be so angry. Maybe all the wishing was finally paying off?

Emme loved maybes.

They strolled a couple of streets over, past the gigantic dry cleaners, Clark's Pharmacy, the Unique Boutique charity shop, Plainway supermarket, a card shop with no name and a number of other places with the lights on inside. Emme's spirits lifted with each crack in the pavement as they got closer to Daisy's.

She was actually skipping by the time they hit the corner.

"Hmm, it doesn't look open," Dad said as they approached the bakery.

"What?" Emme cried, skidding to a halt.

"Well, that's disappointing," Mum said. "I would have thought they'd stay open since it was such a big day for them ..."

"Emme and her friends probably ate them out of business," Dad teased.

Emme ran ahead and planted her palms on the big door. It was only eight o'clock, but Daisy's Desserts was indeed closed up tight for the night. A pale glow of light cast shadows over the interior. Mum and Dad peered inside with Emme. The electricity of earlier in the day seemed to have gone out.

"Cozy," Mum said. "I love the tin signs on the walls. And colourful! This place is terrific."

"It's so annoying!" Emme blurted. "Why isn't it open now? I wanted to show you. You're both here. You're never both here."

"Well, whose fault is that?" Mum said.

Dad gave her a look but ignored her comment. "Maybe the bakery was just done in by the big crowds today," Dad suggested. "Maybe they ran out of sugar …"

"Ran out of *sugar*?" Emme said. "Seriously, Dad? That's a dumb thing to say."

"Emme June!" Mum said. "Don't speak to your father that way."

"Why?" Emme barked back. "That's how *you* talk to him!"

"Em!" Dad cried. "Do not speak to your mother like that."

Emme threw her arms into the air with disgust. Now they were on the same side … against *her*? They didn't understand one thing about this moment, why it was so important, why Emme needed the cookies and the bakery, this place with some kind of *magic* that she knew could make all the difference for the three of them tonight. They didn't get it! This wasn't working out the way she had hoped at all.

Her plans for Operation Anniversary Surprise were falling flat before they even began. No matter what Emme did, everything about this scene would always be fake and awkward, and Mum and Dad would be angry with each other forevermore. All the sticky icing in the world couldn't hold this family together. There was only one solution: leave.

"I'm going home," Emme said, turning on one heel and heading back in the direction of their flat. She imagined her room, her safe haven. This night had started out with so much promise, but now all Emme felt was frustration.

"Emme!" Mum and Dad cried at the same time.

Emme didn't turn back around.

She could feel her trainers lifting up off the pavement as she sped home, like she was on some kind of actual moving walkway, like the people conveyor belts they have at airports. Emme could barely catch her breath, but she didn't stop moving, didn't stop until she got to the brass doors of The Enterprise Building, the oddly science fiction-themed name for their block of flats.

She blew into the sparkling marble-floored entrance and collapsed onto the lobby's couch, sinking fast into the soft leather.

A few moments later, Dad and Mum came rushing in together.

"What was *that*?" Mum cried, trying to catch her breath.

Dad scratched his head, wordless.

Emme pulled herself off the couch, went over to the lifts, and clicked the up arrow.

No one said another word on the ride upstairs.

Pup tarts

On Monday, Emme made a beeline for Daisy's Desserts after school. Something about it just seemed to lure her back. She had this weird feeling that maybe being there would help everything else make sense.

Emme's plan to unite Mum and Dad for a trip to the bakery had failed and the rest of the weekend had gone no better. Mostly Emme just stayed in her room and ate crisps, listened to streaming music, watched lame TV reruns on Netflix and did mounds of homework. Something sugar-sprinkled today would make things so much better.

The bakery was busy, but not anywhere near as news-crew busy as it had been on Friday. Most of the tables were occupied, and there were new tables set outside too. There was a queue of customers waiting by the brass, old-fashioned register that went *ching-ching* every time it rang up a sale. But it wasn't chaos. Just a happy thrum of activity.

Emme didn't see Daisy straight away. Instead, she saw the familiar backside of another baker clearing away drained coffee cups and dishes with crumbs. Emme remembered the name on her apron.

"Dina?" Emme whispered.

Her voice barely squeaked amidst the scuffle and hubbub of all the customers in the shop, but Dina whirled around so fast she nearly lost the grip on her coffee cups.

"Well, hello, you!" Dina said warmly. "You were here for the Grand Opening, right? Sat right over ... there?" She gestured to the table where the girls had been.

"Whoa. You really remember me?"

Dina tapped her forehead. "I remember *everything.* You tried all the samples. Am I right? And when you went home, you collapsed in a whipped-cream coma, am I right?" she repeated with a grin.

"Right," Emme said. That wasn't so far from the truth, but Dina could have said that about anyone who'd been there on Friday. "And actually, I came back on Friday night, to bring my mum and dad. But the bakery was closed."

"Ahhh, yes," Dina shook her head. "We shut the doors at six. There was a bit of excitement in the place. Most unexpected."

"You mean all the cameras?"

Dina leaned close. "Well, dear," she said softly. "You have to understand. Mysterious things *happen* in this place."

"What do you mean?"

"Well, for starters, the power went out in some kind of electric shock."

"Electric?"

"Ah, yes. Well, that's Daisy. Crazy things always

happen when Daisy's around," Dina whispered conspiratorially.

Emme didn't know what to say. What did Dina mean by that?

"Have a seat," Dina said. "I'll get Daisy for you now."

"But I really only came for a cookie ..." Emme trailed off, not wanting to bother Daisy.

But Dina waved a hand and scooted back to the cashier's counter, wiping at crumbs and greeting customers as she went. All around the shop, people noshed on desserts and slurped warm drinks. Beverages were served in fancy mugs of all different colours and sizes. Emme hadn't noticed them before or the enormous row of coffeemakers behind one counter – big copper pots with steam coming out the sides like machines from Willy Wonka's factory.

All at once, Daisy appeared through one of the coffeemaker steam clouds with her wild hair tied back in a plaid ribbon. "Dina says you need me!" she said, smiling warmly. She pulled up a wrought iron chair and leaned back, her frizzy hair popping out of its bun in every direction.

Emme smiled. "Um. Actually … um …" She hadn't told Dina that she needed Daisy, but she realized that's what she'd been thinking.

"Glad you came back! Did you tell all your pals about this place?" Daisy cooed.

Emme had passed out some flyers and wanted to tell Daisy, but instead she felt tongue-tied. Daisy had a smattering of beautiful freckles across her cheeks and down to her chin that Emme wanted to connect like dots. It was a starry constellation map up close.

Daisy wore just the teeniest bit of lip gloss, so her lips blushed pink. Other than that she wore no make-up, yet somehow she glowed. Plus, she was dusted in flour like one of her pastries – it was on her hands and clothes and even in that wonderfully frizzy hair. Daisy was like the cool older sister/funny art teacher/amazing neighbour Emme dreamed of having.

"You came back for more than sugar today, didn't you?" Daisy asked softly. "I can see it in your eyes."

And just like that, there it was. That feeling from before. A zing of hope shot through Emme. How did Daisy know?

"Yeah, I just felt like I needed to come back," Emme admitted. "I really like it here."

Without warning, Dina swooped towards the table and winked as she slid a warm plate towards Emme. "Careful, it's hot and sticky," Dina whispered. Then she disappeared again.

The crisp, brown square dripped with cara-mel goo and golden raisins. Emme could see juicy chunks of apple inside.

"My apple bars are a cure-all," Daisy said, push-ing the plate a bit closer to Emme.

"*Oooh*! Raisins are my favourite." Emme scooped it up and bit into its gooey goodness. "This is the most delicious thing ever. It *is* applicious."

"Did you say 'happy-licious'?" Daisy asked with

a smile. "Because we just happen to specialize in happy. One bite of an apple bar and – see? The look in your eyes just changed."

Emme took another sticky bite. "Did it change some more?" she giggled.

"Mary Poppins said a spoonful of sugar helps the medicine go down. But it's really so much more than that," Daisy explained. "Here's what I think– "

"*Woooooooof!*"

All at once, they were interrupted by the sudden arrival of a huge Irish wolfhound puppy through the front doors of the bakery.

"*RUMMMPFFFFF!*" the dog barked, clearing the front part of the shop as people ducked into corners to avoid him. "*ROOROROORWF!*"

"Oh, no!" Daisy sprang up from her seat. "Excuse me, sir! We can't have dogs inside – sorry!" she called out to the dog's owner. "There's a steel hook outside to tie up your lead if you want to come inside. But that dog has to go."

"He's never done this before! My apologies!" the

dog's owner called out, struggling to control the lead. "I don't know what's come over him!"

Daisy had her hands on her hips now, looking stern, though a small smile crept to the corner of her lips. Emme could tell that Daisy didn't like having to raise her voice like that. But the alternative was a dog running wild in the shop. The deeply apologetic owner dragged his dog back out, the wolfhound eagerly barking and shaking his rear end all the while. The man must have found the steel hook because not two minutes later, he bounded back into the bakery, dog-free. He headed for the back of the shop.

Emme's eyes followed and then she realized there was sign on the back wall that read, "*PUP TARTS*". They had desserts for *dogs*? Daisy's Desserts really had thought of everything.

Emme had missed the entire array of animal crackers and other stuff that was back there – even bone-shaped dog cakes! Emme thought Daisy could probably even make liver cookies taste good.

Although the pup's owner promised the wolf-hound was outside and tied up, it only took a few minutes for the pup to come loose from its lead. It bounded back into the bakery with a louder *row-wwf*. And he was not alone this time! Right behind the wolfhound was a little shih tzu no bigger than a snowball. He yipped bravely at the heels of the wolfhound.

Emme giggled when she noticed the dogs' fur sticking straight up, just like *her* hair had been at the Grand Opening.

"*Noooooooo!*" a cry went out. It was Daisy, leaping towards the pooches. The wolfhound whipped itself around in a full circle, tail wagging excitedly. The shih tzu yapped and skidded under a table, colliding with a small display cabinet.

This was a scene from a TV sitcom. The shop had been turned into a slapstick Rube Goldberg chain reaction. Emme had recently seen a TV programme about Rube Goldberg. He was an American cartoon-ist and inventor in the early 1900s who created all sorts of interesting contraptions that offered comically complicated solutions to everyday tasks. Emme imagined a Rube Goldberg bakery with flying cake tins and rolling tubes of icing, all working like an assembly line to make the best dessert of all time. She giggled to think that that might actually be what went on behind Daisy's kitchen doors.

Today's sequence of events kicked off with a spontaneous tail wag from the wolfhound, who flopped into a flustered customer, who turned around and knocked over a chair, which launched a teacup, which smashed onto the floor and sent chips of porcelain flying, which made everyone start screaming ... and so on. And then there was the little shih tzu, standing on a chair and eating someone's pastry.

Good thing the news reporter wasn't there today.

Even with all the hubbub, Daisy had everything under control in a matter of minutes. Emme saw how easily Daisy was able to transform chaos into calm. Once the pups were banished from the bakery, each one chomping on a delicious and meaty bone-shaped treat as a distraction, she got the staff to help tidy up. Dina set the cabinet cookie display up again. Carlos came out from the back area to survey the damage. Brooms were on the move and dustpans were put to work. Laughing customers returned to their seats, and in no time, the doggy incident was forgotten.

Emme was amazed at how Daisy and her bakery staff worked in synch. It was as if they could all speak another language to one another without saying a word. Emme wanted to speak it too.

When everything was settled, just like that, Daisy came back to Emme's table.

"Now that's what I call excitement," Daisy said with a sigh. "You like dogs?"

"Not anymore," Emme joked. "Actually, I'm more of a fish girl. Do you make cookies for fish?"

Daisy shook her head thoughtfully. "Not yet. Interesting idea though."

"This place is so ..." Emme said. "I don't know what. I was actually feeling a little down in the dumps before."

"And now?" Daisy asked.

Emme took another big bite of Daisy's Amazing Applicious bar.

"*Mmmmmm*," Emme said, licking all the sugary 'medicine' off her lips. "Spoonful of sugar works."

Too many cookies

By the time Friday came back around that week, war had broken out. Emme and Lizzie tried to pretend it wasn't that big a deal. They walked home from school just like any other day. But it wasn't just like any other day. They'd got into a huge fight with their BFF Trish.

"I don't know why she has to act like that," Lizzie said. "And I don't even care if she never talks to me again."

"You don't mean that," Emme said.

"Oh yeah, I really do. She can't just back out of our social studies project like that. I mean, how could she do that to us?"

Emme shrugged. She wanted to defend Trish, but honestly, she didn't know what had happened. Trish had exploded angrily at the two girls that afternoon, saying some surprising things about feeling like an "outsider" and some mean things about Lizzie being "bossy" and "pushy".

"Don't be mad," Emme tried to calm Lizzie as they walked. "You know she isn't usually like that."

"Well, she was like that just now," Lizzie said, kicking a pebble hard. "She hurt my feelings. I told you before."

The week had been stressful with tests lined up almost every day in all subjects and the project in social studies about ancient Egypt. Just a couple of hours ago, it had been a team project with Emme, Lizzie and Trish working together. Now, it was just Emme and Lizzie, because Trish had suddenly dropped out in a huff.

"So what are we going to do now?" Lizzie asked. "We're *three* powerful female rulers from ancient times. How can we do that with only two people?"

They'd called their project "Sisters Across Time". They already had costumes to wear for their presentation, and they were planning to make a poster to use as a visual aid. Each of them worked on a section of the project devoted to a woman leader from ancient times.

Emme was Hatshepsut. Lizzie was Nefertiti. And Trish was Cleopatra. Or at least she *had* been until this afternoon when she changed her mind. Now Trish said she was just going to make a pyramid out of foam instead for her project. Just like that.

"I just don't get why she changed her mind," Emme said. "She blew up at me, and I didn't even do anything."

Emme looked pointedly at Lizzie, but Lizzie just shrugged. Lizzie was never this quiet. Was she hiding something? "Lizzie, tell me the truth. Did *you* say something to Trish?"

"No," Lizzie shrugged. "I mean, I don't know."

Of course Lizzie had said something to Trish, probably something pushy like she'd said last week at the bakery when she teased Trish about the new boy. Lizzie was always talking too much, and it got her into trouble.

Emme frowned. "Tell me everything you said, Lizzie," she demanded.

"I just told Trish that the project wasn't quite there yet, and she hadn't done as much work as we had done, and that the credit for the project was really important."

Emme rolled her eyes. "Lizzie! That was mean and not even true. Just because Trish had volleyball practice that one night and missed our meeting doesn't make her lazy. She's the one who found our costumes! You shouldn't have said that."

"Look, I always tell the truth," Lizzie said, holding up her fingers in the Girl Scout code of honour position. They'd been Scouts together a few years ago, and they still used the special hand signal, especially at moments like this where honour mattered most of all.

"You should keep the truth to yourself if it hurts

somebody. We have to find a way to apologize," Emme said, sounding determined.

"We could go shoe shopping," Lizzie suggested.

"Shoe shopping? How will *that* help?"

"We can forget all about school and our project for now and work out how to make things better with Trish *while we shop*. Trish likes shoes. Doesn't she?"

"Shopping is your answer to everything," Emme said. "But I'm not in the mood for Forever Teen or Très Bien." Those were both shops that specialized in cheap and funky clothes they liked. "Let's stop over at Daisy's Desserts instead. You haven't been back there since the Grand Opening."

"Pastries over shoes?" Lizzie asked. "You really love that bakery, don't you?"

Emme nodded. "Don't you?"

Lizzie shrugged. "It's okay, I suppose, but ... I don't know how to tell you this, Emme, but baked goods are not the key to life."

"Says who?" Emme demanded, not quite joking.

"I ate enough cookies at that grand opening to last me a lifetime. And it's a little crazy there, don't you think?"

"There is no such thing as too many cookies," Emme said. "And I think *you're* crazy."

Lizzie chuckled. "Yeah, whatevs. Don't get all twisted." She ran on ahead of Emme.

By now they'd reached the Enterprise and Emme's very old doorman, Seymour, was there in his black coat, neat black hat and pencil thin mustache to greet them. Seymour looked more like a character from a French film than an ordinary doorman.

He opened the door wide. "Good *ahhhhfternoon*, ladies," he said with a bow.

"Good *ahhhhfternoon*," Lizzie and Emme said at the exact same time, playfully mimicking Seymour's accent like they always did.

Inside the lift, they were talking easily again. Over the years, this was typical between the two of them. They would have a spat about something and realize five minutes later that it was easier to not hold a grudge and just move on. Unfortunately, Trish got too caught up in her anger sometimes, and she didn't know how to let it go.

"I really think you and Trish are overreacting," Lizzie said as they entered Emme's flat with the key that they kept under the bristly doormat. "You two always act like *I'm* inventing all the drama."

"Well?" Emme gave Lizzie a sharp look. "Aren't you?"

Lizzie huffed.

They walked inside the flat and Emme felt a cold draft. The windows were all open, and the cool breeze blew in, billowing the curtains.

"Mum?" Emme called out. No one answered. She felt a pang of worry. "MUM?"

The room reeked of jasmine. The smell hit Emme hard. Mum must have just spritzed room spray all over. Whenever things were getting very

tense at home, Mum went nuts cleaning and tidy-
ing up. Emme knew this meant that Mum probably
wasn't too happy.

From down the hall, Mum appeared, bucket in
hand, scarf wrapped around her head. Yep, she was
at it again.

"Hi, girls," Mum said without much enthusiasm.
"I thought you might have stopped at that bakery
you love so much."

Emme nudged Lizzie. "Nope. Apparently Lizzie
doesn't like cookies anymore."

"That's not what I said!" Lizzie protested. "That
place just has an odd vibe. And like I said, I'm still
full from last week!"

"Right, right," Emme said teasingly.

"*Ooookay*," Mum said, giving the girls a confused
look. "I left some snacks in the kitchen for you,
Emme. There should be enough for both of you. But
don't make a mess. I've been– "

"Cleaning," Emme cut her off. "We can see that.
You okay, Mum?"

Mum gave a tight smile. "Why wouldn't I be?"

Emme and Lizzie grabbed a bowl of popcorn and headed into Emme's room to finish up some work on the project. But with the radio blasting the latest top 40 and every few minutes one of them breaking into song or dance, the homework wasn't really getting done. At least the dancing and singing made Emme forget about the over-sprayed jasmine and overstressed Mum for a while.

After about half an hour with the bedroom door shut, there was a bang. Was that a door? Then Emme and Lizzie heard yelling.

"What is that?" Lizzie asked.

Emme quickly turned down the volume on the radio. The noise came from the living room. Mum was on the phone. Was she shouting? Emme knew Dad was probably on the other end of the line.

Embarrassed, Emme glanced over at Lizzie.

"What's going on? Is everything okay?" Lizzie asked quietly, obviously knowing everything was *not* okay.

"Of course, everything is fine!" Emme lied. She didn't want to get into it, especially after what Lizzie said on Instagram the first time Emme had confided that her parents were fighting.

But it was kind of hard to hide the truth when they could hear Emme's mum yelling things like, "I don't want to talk about this!" and "We are never going to sort this out," and "Don't threaten me!"

"I don't know what this is about," Emme lied. "Maybe that's the plumber. Or the caretaker? I don't know. Mum yells at him a lot."

"Emme, I'm your BFF," Lizzie said. "Tell me the truth."

"I am!" Emme snapped. "Why do you even care?"

Lizzie frowned deeply. "Why wouldn't I care? I am like your best friend on the entire planet."

"*One* of my best friends," Emme corrected her.

Mum was still yelling, and Emme covered her ears. She wanted everything to just stop, including Lizzie's visit. "You should go home," she said to Lizzie.

"What? Why can't you just talk to me? Telling me to go home? That's such a dumb thing to say."

"Dumb thing? Seriously?" Emme clenched her jaw, even though she'd said the very same thing to Dad last week. It was *not* nice. "Now you should definitely go home," she repeated.

"Home?" Lizzie grabbed Emme's arm. "Emme! I didn't say anything wrong. You are totally over-reacting. We should have just gone shoe shopping. You're the one making all the drama now!"

"Please just go," Emme shook off Lizzie. "I'll see you later."

At that exact moment, Mum's voice got louder than ever and Lizzie's eyes got really wide. Emme felt everything shrink in on her – walls, doors, windows. It was hard to catch her breath. Just when things seemed to quiet down, they'd explode out of nowhere. Not only was Emme ashamed that it was happening in front of Lizzie – she was worried about what this argument meant for Mum and Dad.

"Okay, I'll go," Lizzie said quietly. She gathered

up the books that they'd barely looked at. Emme just watched as Lizzie re-packed her bag and put on her jacket.

"See you at school, right?" Lizzie asked as they walked out of the room and to the front door.

"Right," Emme said simply.

"Wait! What about our project?" Lizzie asked.

"Let's just finish our sections on our own. And we can talk to Trish Monday at school. We'll apologize for the whole fight. She'll get over it. Okay? It'll be fine. Bye."

"Okay. Bye," Lizzie murmured.

After re-locking the door behind Lizzie, Emme headed back to her room. Mum appeared, shaking her head. Her face was splotchy pink.

"Your father has to leave for another business trip. He'll be gone on our anniversary *again*. We have tried, Emme, but I'm so sorry honey ... this can't go on."

Emme's heart was in her throat. She had thought she'd have more time. Her mind raced. If she was hoping to get a surprise in order for Mum and Dad's special day, she would have to think minnow-fast. Now it seemed the surprise might have to happen *before* the actual anniversary! It would have to be something so spectacular, so original, that it would make them fall instantly back in love.

She'd started to lose faith the other night, but suddenly she felt more determined than ever.

She needed a serious plan.

She needed bigger – and *sweeter* – ideas.

Who was she kidding? She needed a magic wand.

Chapter 6

A dose of delicious

Sunday evening Emme sat at her computer. The sun set, leaving her room in darkness while she worked. Soon the only light came from her screen, sending a cool glow all over her blue room and making it seem even more like an ocean. She felt like she was underwater, separate from the rest of the world.

A plan to keep Mum and Dad together was in order. But what to do? Emme scrolled through different websites looking for ideas with a variety of Internet searches.

Anniversary party

Treating your parents

Happy anniversary mum and dad

And the last one, which Emme typed in desperately:

Stop divorce from happening

Usually for the anniversary surprise, Emme lit candles, prepared a song or speech, told some ridiculous jokes or choreographed a short dance routine that she performed in the living room. This year Emme needed to do something bigger. But the ideas posted online for anniversaries were way too complicated for what Emme could afford or make happen in such a short time. She'd earned some money from being a babysitter for families in her block – the Hidalgos on the sixth floor (two crazy children) and the Westerleys on the tenth (one very spoiled child). She glanced at the calendar and in her secret stash of cash. She had nine days and £70.

Emme kept surfing around. She found her fingers typing a familiar name into one of the search engines: Daisy's Desserts.

Instantly a web address popped up. Emme hit

the hyperlink. With a poof of pink, the website for Daisy's Desserts appeared on screen. The masthead read: THE DESSERT DIARIES. Emme leaned back and traced the cupcake cursor around the screen.

Of course – Daisy's! There was so much to look at. Right at the top was a greeting and a recent blog entry.

Emme clicked on it.

Dear Sweeties,

They're here, at last, and no deep fryer's big enough to hold the dozens and dozens I'm ready to make: doughnuts! I've been planning my next big attack on the baking world, and I think the best thing to debut is the almighty doughnut. I never had a dilemma a doughnut didn't solve, did you? Working on flavours now – if you have ideas, click below and send me an email. Lemon coconut cream, anyone?

Daisy

Emme broke into a wide grin. It was as if Daisy was sitting right here with her in the bedroom, chatting about things they both loved. There was a whole archive of posts from the past several

months. Daisy had been posting entries before she even opened up Daisy's Desserts.

Dear Sweeties,

For the last three hours, I have polished, wiped, cleaned and set up this bakery. From the street it looks like nothing, just an empty shopfront and some paper on the windows. But inside things are really cooking! I'm already on my third cup of coffee (from our brand-new espresso maker, I might add), and my stomach is stretched from taste-testing no fewer than ten versions of the almost-famous apple bars. BUT I am right here, doing exactly what I'm meant to be doing. Look into your heart of hearts. Do you have a secret wish hiding there? A word to the wise — my apple bars have a way of making the truth come out!

Thankfully Dina is working the ovens with Carlos. My two best friends in the universe — now my business partners. We all believe in the power of pastry and some sprinkles. And why not? Carlos was runner-up last season on that TV reality show *Baked Good*. I taught him how to make his very first raspberry soufflé, I'll have you know! Lately, though, I'm more into cupcakes.

My lovely Nana Belle is to blame (or credit!) for

all this sugar and flour! When I was a little girl, she used to hum this song, "Life is Sweet", and roll out the pie dough. I remember the way her kitchen smelled – like cocoa and cinnamon and warm bread. Nana believed she could bake love into everything. And so she could.

Now it's my turn. I hope maybe this shop can bring a little dose of delicious to this neighbourhood. I believe in Nana Belle and the possibility of a good crust and something chewy and fourteen kinds of cookies. Don't you?

Thank you for reading my Dessert Diaries! And come and see me at Daisy's Desserts ... opening SOON!

xo, Daisy

Emme read through dozens of the blog entries for Daisy's Desserts. She learned a lot about how the bakery had come to be and who worked there and what was planned for the future. Daisy's menu on the blog's homepage was chock-full of creative ideas and photographs. How was it possible that that one frizzy head had so many amazing ideas percolating inside of it? Best of all was the feeling Emme got from reading Daisy's words. That electricity from the bakery even hummed through her writing and made Emme feel that everything, somehow, would be okay.

mmmmmENU
All About Daisy
The Dessert Diaries Blog
Recipe Station
New & Different on the Menu
The Impossible List of Cupcake Flavours
Top It Off Cupcake Party Tips
Photo Gallery
Food Fairs and Other Events (coming soon!)
Safety & Allergies
Can I Order Daisy's Apple Bars Online? (Yes!)
Contact (Submit a Half-Baked Idea)

Some parts of the website were still "in progress", so there was a lot to look forward to reading in the future. Emme was impressed – even starstruck. Daisy certainly was a busy person. How did she have time to bake so many delicious things, set up an exciting new bakery and reach out to people online? Did she ever sleep? Maybe that was why her hair was always so crazy?

Emme knew she had to get back to her anniversary mission, but she found the website somehow comforting – and addictive! There was enough stuff to click on to keep Emme reading for days. Daisy had even posted some funny childhood anecdotes and photos along with her biography. Emme clicked.

DAISY DUNCAN. PROPRIETOR. DAISY'S DESSERTS

Daisy was born on a farm in the middle of nowhere. She used to collect eggs from three special chickens (Fern, Lacy and Gilda) and bring them to her Nana Belle, who taught Daisy how to cook her very first mini-cake. From the moment that springy chocolate creation came out of the oven, Daisy was hooked on baking. In addition to the sweets, Daisy fancies herself as a savoury chef too, as needed. But sweets are her specialities!

Experience: baking apprentice to Master Chef and Patisserie Owner Jean-Claude Cocteaux; freelance event planner/caterer for "Ganache on the Go"; and flea market regular at Common Grounds.

Daisy sometimes wishes she lived in a big barn

but she for now lives in the city with her pet gecko.

As Emme clicked through more of the site, she thought about how Daisy must have spent a very long time dreaming up what her business would be like. There really was magic in it – in all of it. Emme found a blog entry that was posted just after the Grand Opening. She couldn't believe what was right there in black, white (and pink) on the web page – something very familiar.

Dear Sweeties,

What a day – OPENING DAY!!! A sugar-coated, crowded-to-the-rafters kind of day! The news crew made it. so Daisy's is now broadcast across the area. (Thanks, Babs, for setting that up.) I expect it will help with business, although after today's turnout, the only help I need is getting more eggs, butter and sugar into my refrigerators!

I can't believe how many people came out to support us. I am so grateful. On behalf of Carlos, Dina, Babs and the rest of our baking crew:
WE ♡ YOU!

Overheard today in my bakery:

"There's so much chocolate in this fudge chip lava cupcake that I think I need a chocolate intervention." (Daisy Duncan, MD, as in Majorly Delicious, at your service)

"This place is exactly what this neighbourhood needs." (My sentiments exactly.)

"I want to steal everything." (Sample, yes. Steal, no. Please pay the nice lady at the pretty brass cash register, thank you very much.)

"There's got to be some kind of magic going on here ..." (Emme and her two pals from the school around the corner, who staked out a table and settled in permanently)

"Where have you been all my life?" (Senior citizen who proposed marriage after three apple bars)

Well, time to flake off like the best kind of pie crust. Be back real soon!

xo, Daisy

Emme was famous! Well, not exactly famous, but it was her first appearance on a blog of any kind. She liked the fact that she'd made it a blog that was measured in teaspoons of baking powder and chocolate nibs. Maybe it was a sign that one day Emme herself would be baking ... and creating world peace through pastries? When she wasn't deep-sea diving and saving the whales, of course.

Emme didn't want to get too carried away, but it *was* an exciting moment. She loved seeing her name right there on the screen, as if Daisy had whispered some kind of personal message to her, as if Emme were now a part of some secret society. It was enough to give her the good kind of goosebumps.

What was truly amazing about this moment, however, was that Emme had realized Daisy's Desserts was not only a cool bakery with an even cooler baker called Daisy. It was more than just a building and a place to buy cookies or dog-bone-shaped pet treats. Daisy's Desserts might just be the key to making Mum and Dad's anniversary celebration the best one ever!

The bakery had been closed when Mum and Dad tried to visit before, but that was just a fluke. Daisy definitely was the right person to help Emme plan the event of a lifetime, a celebration that just might, *maybe*, if she was very, very lucky, help Emme keep Mum and Dad together forever.

Emme considered clicking the "Contact" button, but that was silly! The bakery was just a few minutes away. Emme knew Daisy up close and personal now. She didn't need an email. She needed to march right over to the bakery.

Emme was ready to ask for help – at last.

And when she went back tomorrow, Emme could also grab another warm apple bar.

Just because.

Chapter 7

Lucky thirteen

It is awkward to juggle angry people. Emme knew that better than anyone.

On Monday morning Trish was still giving Emme and Lizzie the silent treatment. She hadn't got over *anything*. And Lizzie was giving Emme plenty of space after their blow-up at Emme's flat on Friday.

So at lunchtime Emme sat by herself at the yellow table while Trish went to the green table and Lizzie sat at the orange table. Lunch was pretty much the only time they could really socialize, and they still had to prepare for their project. But in order to do that, they needed to be speaking to each other.

That stupid project, Emme thought. It was easier

to blame it for the source of all this conflict instead of the actual reasons.

The social studies teacher, Mr Durke, said the threesome – despite personal grievances – would have to complete the Sisters Across Time project together as assigned, no matter what. He absolutely wouldn't accept a last-minute change of any kind. So they *had* to work out a way to make peace.

When Emme went to the toilet after lunch, she got her chance. There was Trish, washing her hands.

"Hi," Emme said when she saw her.

"Oh, hi," Trish said without her usual enthusiasm.

"Trish," Emme said and then stopped and peered under the stalls. She wanted to make sure they didn't have an audience. "Good, we're alone. Look, I'm sorry for what Lizzie said and did. She was wrong to say that stuff. And I should have called you this weekend, but I was sort of– "

"You have no idea how much Lizzie hurt my

feelings," Trish cut in. She tossed her paper towel in the rubbish and met Emme's eyes in the mirror.

"I know she said you hadn't done as much work on our project," Emme said. "That was kind of mean."

"It was!" Trish said. "But she also said some other stuff. And she texted me too."

"What other stuff?" Emme asked.

"She sent me a text, but I think she meant to send it to you," Trish said. "I didn't tell you before because I was so mad."

Emme felt a lump in her throat. *Uh-oh.* "What did the text say?"

"It said, 'What is her prob she is *sooooo* annoying ALL THE time,'" Trish said in her best Lizzie impression.

Emme shook her head. "Ugh," she said. "Look, I know Lizzie talks and obviously texts too much and sometimes things come out of her mouth – and thumbs – before she thinks."

"No, she's just mean," Trish shook her head.

"And she told on me."

"Told what?" Emme was beginning to realize that the most recent argument was just the tip of the iceberg. It sounded like there had been a lot of reasons for Trish to get upset. Maybe Lizzie was more in the wrong than Emme thought.

"Remember I was telling you about that boy in my block, the one I see in the lift? Bryan?"

Emme nodded. She wondered where this conversation was headed.

"Well, Lizzie saw Bryan by the locker rooms, and she told him that I liked him! So Bryan's twin sister – you know her, right? Molly? She's in our science lesson. Anyway, she keeps giving me dirty looks. And her friends laugh when they pass me in the corridor! Last week they even made fun of my clothes!"

"But they do that to everyone," Emme said. "They *are* mean."

"No, I think Lizzie put them up to it."

"Hold on. You think Lizzie said something to those girls about you?" Emme asked. Her head was spinning. "Like what? She's your friend. She wouldn't do that."

Trish shrugged. "I thought maybe Bryan liked me a little. But now he's ignoring me, and those girls are giving me bad looks. And Lizzie's being mean to me. You connect the dots."

"Trish," Emme groaned. "Come on. Lizzie can be annoying, but this?"

"Right!" Trish said. "That's why I'm so mad! It's like she said something bad about me so that Bryan would like *her* instead."

"So, you really like him?" Emme asked cautiously.

"I don't know," Trish said. She gulped on the last part, which meant that of course she liked him.

Emme knew this was a tricky situation. "If people are saying untrue stuff, you should tell a teacher what is going on," she said. "And maybe you should talk to Bryan yourself to stop any rumours."

Trish laughed. "Oh, yeah, sure. That won't make me a weirdo or anything."

"I don't know what else to tell you," Emme said.

"Forget it," Trish sighed. "I know you're trying to help, but ..."

Emme wanted to give Trish a hug. She wished she could say something that might make the situation better, but she was out of ideas.

Trish hung her head and inhaled deeply. "I better get to my lesson," she said and headed for the door.

Frustrated, Emme blurted out, "Wait! You have to forget all this stuff with the boy. And whatever Lizzie said. At least until the project so we can all get full credit. We need you, Trish."

"I know," Trish said, turning around as she pulled open the door. "I have the Cleopatra costume and my section of the report. I'll be in class on the day we present to do my part. I won't screw it up for anyone, especially not you. Don't worry, okay?"

"I'm sorry about everything," Emme said. "We'll sort out a solution. Are you sure you don't want me to ask Lizzie to apologize or do something?"

"I'm not ready to stop being mad at her," Trish admitted. "Don't say anything."

"Okay," Emme agreed. She wanted to say something else, something more, about the other things that had been going on in her life. She wanted to tell Trish about Mum and Dad and the fighting at home. Trish would know what to say since she'd lived through parents splitting up too.

But before she could say anything, another pair of girls squeezed into the toilets, and Trish went out without another word.

Emme headed to her next lesson. She had so much on her mind these days. Maybe Daisy had some baked wisdom about all this? Today when she went to talk to Daisy about the anniversary, she'd tell her about this too. Daisy probably had a lot to say about friendship troubles. Maybe a little expert wisdom was the one missing ingredient Emme needed to make up (bake up?) with her friends.

But then again, Emme felt like she didn't have any spare time to worry about her friends. She had all she could manage planning Mum and Dad's perfect anniversary. There was work to be done, and Emme had to stay focused! After school, she made a beeline for Daisy's Desserts with one goal in mind. If the friendship stuff came up, she'd ask Daisy about that too. But the primary objective was OPERATION ANNIVERSARY SURPRISE!

Daisy was behind the counter today at the bakery, her hair pulled into a beautiful plaited bun with a ribbon and beads woven into it. Daisy was a grown-up, but she was also terribly cool, like a character from a novel, like the fun aunt who comes for visits with a million tiny gifts at the bottom of her bottomless bag.

"It's you!" Daisy called out as soon as she saw Emme.

Emme blushed a little. "You're famous," she said shyly. "I've seen the bakery on the news at least three times."

"That's because the news director at the TV station is addicted to our apple bars. I can't help that," Daisy said, chuckling. "But we're a bit quieter today I'd say. Which is actually a relief. I could use a break. My dogs are tired."

"Your dogs?" Emme looked confused.

"My feet!" Daisy exclaimed and kicked one shoe up into the air. She had on purple shoes with little wedge heels. "Being a fashion plate is exhausting!" she joked. "Ooh, speaking of plates," Daisy said. "Let's get one and fill it up with goodies!"

Emme eyed the treasure chest of baked goods inside the enormous glass display case. She studied the chalkboard menu too. It changed from day to day depending on what Daisy felt like baking.

There were all kinds of cakes today: mud, patty, orange glazed, pound and banana. Cookies took up one entire side of the menu: chocolate chunky, nutty butter surprise, snickerdoodles, butterscotch dots and a dozen others, all of which sounded like heaven. Cupcakes were iced with vanilla, cocoa, cream cheese and other yummy flavours in pink blush, deep blue, sunshine-yellow and even polka dots – Emme's favourite. Daisy had scribbled three items that were "Daisy's Picks" on her chalkboard, including the Applicious Bars (of course), Fudge Doughnuts (a test, Daisy said, in her recent quest to become Doughnut Queen), and Peekaboo Pie (which included whipped cream, chocolate, toffee pieces, biscuits and golden roasted marshmallows).

Emme read the antique tin signs with funny sayings on Daisy's walls. One shaped like a tooth with the word *SWEET* on top. One said *TRUCKERS WELCOME!* and showed a man holding a doughnut like a steering wheel. Another that looked like it had actual rust on it said *R&H Baking Powder Stays Fresh!* And there were loads of *JAVA* and *COFFEE TIME* signs near the enormous coffee machine with the foam and espresso extensions. In addition to the fancier machines, Daisy also had good old ordinary pots of coffee with names like Hawaiian Dark Brew and Guatemalan Cafe Extraordinaire.

"How long have you been collecting this stuff?"

Emme asked, squinting to read a vintage diner menu sign.

"Just about my whole life," Daisy said as she rearranged the muffin display. "My dad and mum had a café and grocery in the small town I grew up in. Before opening here, I shopped for antiques in that area so I could get some original wooden serving cases and signs to decorate. I wanted this place to feel like a piece of the country that just sprouted up in the middle of the city."

"You succeeded!" Emme declared. Everything about Daisy's Desserts felt authentic, right down to the hundred varieties of antique wedding cake toppers on display in another cabinet. Even the wooden chairs felt like they'd just been lifted from someone's old barn or garden. Some were splattered with droplets of paint or the legs were a bit loose, like inside a genuine farmhouse.

Emme's gaze fell upon an oversized glass bell jar at the end of one counter. Inside were pink, green and yellow macarons, piled high.

"Ah, those were my Nana Belle's original recipe," Daisy said with a nod. "Macarons. Have you ever tried one? They are my favourite. Well, *one* of my favourites," Daisy laughed and gave a helpless shrug.

Emme was enraptured by Daisy's every word. But apparently, so was half the neighbourhood. While they'd been talking, people buzzed around Daisy like bees gathering nectar. Daisy answered questions, gave instructions and offered friendly responses to staff and customers. But after each interruption, Daisy gave Emme a secret smile that seemed to say, "Now, back to you, my dear!"

"Daisy, I need to speak with you please," called out one old woman with a carved cane. She was dressed up in a fancy wool suit and wore a hat and gloves. "About that thing you told me last time ..."

"Daisy, where is that new box of supplies?"

"Daisy, I'll be calling you to cater my daughter's wedding. Talk soon!"

"Congratulations, Miss Daisy, for perfection,"

one customer bellowed as he put on his hat. "When I eat your cakes, I feel like singing!" And then he burst into an operatic solo without warning, and soon the entire bakery joined him.

When the singing (and laughing) died down, Daisy laid a hand on Emme's shoulder. "So I know you're not here to sing. It's time for my break. Let's go and chat, shall we?" They found a corner table, and Daisy brought over two glasses of lemon water. "Let's have it."

"Well," Emme said, a little nervously. "I see how you are so nice to everyone, and you know the right thing to say and the perfect dessert to make for every occasion ..."

"Don't mind if I accept that compliment!" Daisy said with a grin.

Emme bit her lip. "Well, here's the thing. I want to make my parents' thirteenth anniversary the best one ever," she said and crossed her fingers under the table for luck.

"Oh," Daisy said excitedly. "Well that is just about

the sweetest thing I can think of! You are a very thoughtful daughter. So, what do they like best?"

"Um," Emme said. "I don't know. Me?" she giggled sheepishly.

"Well, of course! But baked Emmes never come out right for me," Daisy teased. She tapped her chin, thinking. "I could do some chocolate dipped berries for you, or a white cake that looks like a miniature wedding cake perhaps?"

"Hmm," Emme was thinking hard.

These were all great ideas but there was something more she had to say. It was like she *needed* to share. She couldn't hold it in. Something was making her talk.

"What else?" Daisy asked. "What do they like to do together?"

"Well," Emme paused. "Not much. Anymore. I mean, Dad works a lot."

"Hmmm," Daisy said, nodding her head thoughtfully.

"You see," Emme's voice trailed off a little bit.

"They don't really go out on dates since Dad works and travels a lot and Mum is kind of, well, upset a lot. I was hoping I could make this a happy time for them. Like, if I can help to celebrate their anniversary in a new way, things will get better."

"I see," Daisy nodded again.

"You can help me do that right, can't you?" Emme pleaded. "You seem to know how to make things happen and how to make people feel good about themselves. I saw those people singing. Even *I* was singing!"

Daisy laughed. "And you have a lovely voice!"

"That's how you make me feel every time I come into this place." Emme's words came out in a whisper.

Daisy leaned back a little bit in her chair and crossed her arms. "You're a real sweetheart, you know that? Okay, now let's get down to business." She took out her smartphone and started tapping away. Emme leaned over to see what she was typing.

ANNIVERSARY YEARS.

"Thirteen you said, huh?" Daisy asked with a chuckle.

"Yes, but ..." Emme's jaw dropped. "Oh, I wasn't even thinking about unlucky numbers. That's not a good sign, is it?"

"Don't give me any of that unlucky talk!" Daisy shook her head, which made her dangly earrings jingle. "Each person makes his or her own luck. So it says here that the thirteenth anniversary gift of choice is lace. Hmm."

"Lace is fabric. What does that have to do with food?" Emme felt her hopes deflating. "A lace tablecloth?" she suggested lamely.

Daisy's brows furrowed. She was thinking hard but with a twinkle in her eye. Suddenly, she lit up. "I know! My Nana Belle had a recipe that she treasured more than any others. It's just the thing for you – and your parents."

"Is it better than lace?" Emme asked.

"It *is* lace!" Daisy squealed excitedly. "We can

bake Nana's old recipe for lace cookies. She won awards for this recipe. Oh, this is going to be a lot of fun!"

"Lace cookies sound so fancy!" Emme said, her excitement beginning to grow again. She thought of the lace from her mother's wedding veil. Surely this was a good sign!

"Yes!" Daisy laughed. "We'll add magical spun sugar on top too. Your mother and father will love it."

Emme imagined the whole scene in her mind. She'd make dinner for them – nothing too complicated. (She was a good cook, but not *that* good. Not yet anyway!) Maybe she could get fresh pasta and the yummy meatballs from Villarina Trattoria that Dad liked. And she could warm up the homemade tomato sauce that Mum had in the freezer. It was Mum's speciality, and Emme had helped her to make it a few weeks ago. Villarina Trattoria also made a *dee-lish* loaf of Italian bread with amazing garlic butter.

Emme was hungry just thinking about it.

And she could use the fancy crystal glasses and cloth napkins too – the ones with the little embroidered Rs for Remmers. That would make the whole evening even better – as if they were dining in an expensive restaurant. And yes, why not a lace tablecloth?

And she had a bunch of votive candles to light and set the mood for an anniversary theme. Emme wondered if she had thirteen that she could use like anniversary candles instead of birthday candles. She would have to check.

And maybe Emme could borrow Mum's music playlist or download old people music? (Well, not *old* people, exactly, but music from when Mum and Dad were teenagers.) She'd have to think about what would make for the most romantic impact.

Everything had to be perfect, of course. It just had to be. She was like Cupid, delivering love and happiness and lace cookies.

Soon, things would go right back to the way they used to be when she was little.

It gave Emme hope to think of what a little spun sugar might do.

Chapter 8

Home sweet home

Since Emme had been planning the entertainment for Mum and Dad's anniversary for so many years, she had a list of things she always did. One: decorate with a theme. Two: make a fancy programme that looked like a real playbill. Three: make a homemade card with love and thank yous.

But what would she do for this big anniversary party and show? This was the most important one ever. Emme knew that Mum and Dad hardly even spoke these days. She knew how angry Mum felt and how distant Dad seemed. He was on the road working half the time. Could Emme make something so beautiful and funny for them that they would forget all the bad stuff and remember all the good times?

Emme missed Dad when he was gone so much. He texted her goodnight every night that he wasn't home, but it wasn't the same. What she missed most, though, was that feeling she had when they were all together. It was like they were all three connected with a strong thread that no one could break. No matter how far one person went, the other two would be right by his or her side. Emme missed *that* feeling.

On Friday afternoon, to get inspired for the big anniversary reunion, Emme went down to the basement of their block of flats and dug into storage space 102. That was where Mum and Dad stored Christmas decorations and fake Halloween pumpkins and things like the inflatable raft they took to the country in the summer. After some rummaging, Emme found what she was looking for: the box of photo albums that Mum had made over the years.

Emme dragged the box upstairs so she could

look through it. She hid it in her bedroom so Mum wouldn't catch her flipping through all the prized family pics.

Inside one book were loads of very old snapshots of Mum and Dad from the day they were married and their honeymoon after that. Emme poured over the pages one by one, trying to imagine how things had happened the way they did. There were photos of Mum and Dad on holiday, skiing, on a plane to somewhere far, far away. Every moment had a story.

That was it! Emme would use the programme to get Mum and Dad to tell the stories of their years together and keep those stories alive. It was a perfect thing to talk about on their anniversary.

The phone rang while Emme was working on the programme. "Hello?" she said cheerily, happy that her plan was falling into place.

"Hi," the voice on the other end sounded a bit hoarse. But Emme knew who it was right off the bat.

"Lizzie? What's up?"

"Nothing."

"Nothing? Wait, you called me."

"Yeah," Lizzie stammered. "I'm in the lobby. Can I come up?"

There was a scuffling noise and the phone receiver sounded like static.

"Okay," Emme said. "Come on up."

Mum was at work, but she wouldn't mind. Dad was working too, as usual. Emme and Lizzie *definitely* needed to talk.

Emme pushed the buzzer to let Lizzie in, and soon she was at the door. Emme flung it open, eager to hear what was going on. Emme hadn't really spoken to either Lizzie or Trish except for when they were in front of Mr Durke's class on Wednesday, presenting Sisters Across Time. But that didn't really count as talking to each other. (And Mr Durke seemed to agree – he'd given them a C on the presentation for "lack of preparation and teamwork". Sigh. So much for Emme's good grades.)

"Hi!" Emme said, curious to see what Lizzie had on her mind. "Long time no see."

"Long time," Lizzie agreed and gave a small smile. "I remembered about your anniversary project and came over to see if you needed any help."

"Yes please!" Emme said, and any awkwardness from the last week was swept away.

"Can I have a snack?" Lizzie asked, making herself at home, as usual.

Emme laughed and they headed towards the kitchen, but the phone rang so Emme told Lizzie to help herself to the snacks.

"Hi, honey." It was Mum.

"Hi, Lizzie came by," Emme said. "So we're just hanging out. Is that okay?"

"Of course, that's fine. Just take the frozen chicken out of the freezer for me, okay?" Mum asked.

Buzzzzzzzz.

Emme jumped. It was the lobby buzzer again.

"Got it, Mum. Gotta run!"

"Someone else here to see you, Miss," Seymour said when Emme hit the intercom. "It's Mademoiselle Trish," he said with his usual humorous formality, as if they lived in some millionaire building and not just The Enterprise.

Emme's eyes went wide, stunned. *Trish? Here? What?*

"Was that the buzzer?" Lizzie asked, coming out of the kitchen with crisps and an apple.

Emme nodded nervously. "It's Trish."

"What? Seriously? Did you plan this?"

Emme shook her head. "No, I swear. She doesn't even know you're here."

"She sent me a text and said she's not mad anymore," Lizzie said, "but I feel terrible about what happened. What am I supposed to say now? This is too weird."

"Did you say you were sorry – those exact words?" Emme asked. "Tell me what you told her."

"Well, I sort of told her sorry," Lizzie said sheepishly.

"Sort of?" Emme knew what that meant. Lizzie had a habit of only telling *part* of a story. And she was not very good at saying sorry.

"What happened?" Emme asked matter-of-factly. "Tell me. Quick, before Trish comes up."

Lizzie shrugged. "I apologized about the Bryan thing. Total misunderstanding. But now there's a slight possibility that I might have offended her again. I said something, and she got all twisted. And it was not a big deal, I swear. I only insulted *one* part of her outfit, not the whole thing. But if she dressed better, Bryan might pay her more attention!"

"Seriously?" Emme put her head in her hands. "What did you say?"

"I just told her that her shirt was kind of a mess."

"You did *not* say that."

"But it was true!" Lizzie protested.

"This whole thing is 'kind of a mess'!" Emme said, throwing her hands into the air as the bell rang. She peered through the peephole in the door.

"Hi, Trish," Emme said, opening the door.

"Hi, yourself," Trish strolled in.

"Trish!" Lizzie yelled with a bit of false cheer. "What are you doing here?"

Trish shot a look at Emme. "I came because I knew Em needed help with her anniversary project. I remembered she mentioned it last week last at lunch."

"Well," said Lizzie, "me too!"

"You can both help!" Emme declared. "Okay? No fighting? No weirdness? I need you two today." And then Emme told them about the problems with her parents.

Everyone got quiet.

"We're here for you," Trish said. Lizzie nodded.

They all sat down on the floor and began to page through the photo albums. It was fun to invent their own stories about why people were in certain places and why they were wearing such funny clothes and hairstyles.

With the three of them looking at things together, the ideas for the programme multiplied.

They shared a few belly laughs too. It almost seemed like old times.

"Your mum was so pretty," Trish remarked.

"She still is pretty," Lizzie said.

"Yeah," Emme mused, looking at a photo of her mum's beautiful black hair blowing in the breeze.

Trish grabbed a pencil, sharpened it and began to sketch on a white sheet of paper. She was making a drawing of a couch with a couple seated on it. Lizzie grabbed a few of the photographs that she'd just dug out of the box and arranged them collage-style for the middle of the programme. Now it was really starting to come together.

"You're a really good artist, T," Emme said. Trish had drawn the outline of a layer cake. There were all sorts of things flying in the sky. Butterflies! Hundreds of butterflies meant lots of changes all happening at the same time. The butterfly was a symbol of transformation. And hope, Emme decided to believe.

Time flew as Trish shaded in areas and put the finishing touches on the programme art.

Emme dreamed up a poem for the inside and copied it down carefully.

> *Happy Anniversary time is here*
> *You are both so very dear*
> *I made you something really great*
> *I don't want you to separate*
> *Please stay together all the time*
> *And I will call you all mine*

"The last line doesn't quite rhyme," Lizzie pointed out.

"Yeah, and I probably shouldn't say that line about separating. That can't stay in," Emme thought out loud. She went back to fix it while Trish and Lizzie worked some more on the art and photographs. It only took a few more minutes to revise her poem.

> *Happy Anniversary time is here*
> *You are both so very dear*
> *I want you both to celebrate*
> *Mum and Dad, I cannot wait*

I have so much love to show
You will never want to go
Anywhere but home sweet home
That is why I wrote this poem.

"That's so perfect!" Trish cried out. "Emme it's so good that you were honest. You actually said 'don't go'. Maybe your Dad will get it."

Emme shrugged. "Maybe."

"I'm sorry," Lizzie blurted out of nowhere. "Really sorry."

Trish looked at Emme.

Emme looked at Trish.

"You're sorry?" Trish asked. Neither she nor Emme had ever heard Lizzie officially apologize for anything before this moment.

"I really miss this. I miss you two," Lizzie said.

Everyone was still and quiet again.

Then Emme said, "I miss you both too. I know I've been down and acting weird lately because of all this stuff with my parents. I know I'm responsible for some of the drama."

"Me too," Trish added. "I think we all are responsible. We got into a fight that doesn't even make any sense."

"It's so crazy that talking about my parents fighting can bring us closer together."

"They're gonna love this programme," Trish said, trying to sound hopeful.

"Yeah," Lizzie added. "It's going to be great, Emme."

Emme's breath caught in her chest and for a moment she felt woozy. All at once, everything she'd been holding onto inside, keeping secrets from the outside world, all came pouring out in tears. Lizzie and Trish just grabbed Emme and held on.

Emme broke away first. "I missed you – I missed *us – sooooooo* much."

After a minute, Emme sniffed, pulled away and offered her friends a weak smile. "I think we can safely talk about something else now," she said, wiping her nose.

"Like Bryan?" Lizzie asked, teasing.

"Anything but that!" Trish shrieked and gave Lizzie a playful shove. "But hey, at least his sister and her friends have stopped whispering about me," Trish said with relief.

"Well that's good news," Emme said, newly optimistic, sniffles disappearing.

They turned on some music and began dancing around the room.

"I love this song!" Trish said, flipping her hair.

"Oh, I heard something juicy," Lizzie said. "Carmen Rodriguez got picked to star on some new reality TV programme!"

"No way!" Emme said.

"I bet she's going to be famous," Trish said, eyes wide.

"She's so lucky!" Lizzie whined.

"Hey, did you see the class election posters?" Trish asked. "Some super-clever girl called Kiki is running for class president. Do you know her? I heard she's taking some college classes! Who has time for extra homework? She sounds nerdy."

Emme smacked Trish's arm for saying that. "*You're* nerdy!"

"You may be a smart nerd too, Emme, but you're also a trendsetter," Lizzie said. "Some other kids have started going to Daisy's Desserts," she continued. "And you were the first to discover that place!"

"Well, I handed out about thirty flyers at school, so I'm glad they worked! It's the least I can do for Daisy." Emme told her friends how she'd reached out to Daisy for help with the anniversary celebration, and she described the lace cookies and the rest of her plan.

"It's just gotta work, Emme!" Lizzie said, clapping.

Emme felt light and happy for the first time in a long time. Her friends were gossiping and laughing again like normal. And with Daisy's magical help, maybe there was even hope for a "happily ever after" for her parents.

Lizzie and Trish pretended to be DJs while

Emme did some kind of goofy pirouette in the middle of the floor.

Then the girls heard a key in the front door lock. Someone was home? *Noooo!*

Quickly, they rushed to gather any of the loose photographs that had been left on the floor. They threw them into a brown box and picked up all of the coloured pencils and other supplies.

Emme tucked the programme draft under couch cushions just as Mum came into the living room and dropped her stuff on the chair, clearly tired. Things were still a bit of a mess, but she didn't suspect a thing. She seemed happy to see Emme, Trish and Lizzie all in the same room.

"You three are so lucky," Mum said, smiling. "Friendships take work. You girls put in the time. Well done."

"Yeah," Emme said. "We do ... most of the time." She sneaked a sideways glance at her friends, who stifled giggles. If only Mum knew just how much time they'd put into it this week.

"Unfortunately," Mum said, "I'm afraid I have to break up this lovefest. Time for you to go. We need to do a few things around the house."

"I do?" Emme prayed it wouldn't have to do with vacuuming or folding or – blech – *toilets*.

After they'd said their goodbyes and Trish and Lizzie were gone, Mum asked Emme to take a seat on the couch. Emme dropped down and looked up at Mum cautiously.

"What's the matter?" Emme asked, even though deep down she had a hunch about what Mum would say, something she'd been dreading for a while.

"Honey," she started. Emme's stomach lurched a little bit. She knew what was coming. She was desperate to stop the words from being said, but there was nothing she could do.

"Dad and I are going to try living apart for a little while. I know you've suspected this for some time."

Emme's face drooped. Of course she had suspected this – for months. But hearing the words right out here in the open stung hard. Those tears and that lump in her throat that had been hovering just below the surface threatened to come back.

Emme said nothing. How she wished her friends were still here!

"Emme?" Mum asked.

Emme sighed, holding back another flood of tears. She didn't know how she could have any left. It had been one flood after another lately, it seemed.

"Do you have any questions?" Mum asked gently.

Emme shook her head.

"Is there anything you want to say to me?" Mum tried again.

Emme shook her head even harder.

"Well, I'll leave you alone then. We can talk more later. I'll phone for takeaway. You hungry?"

Emme shook her head again. How could she be hungry right now? Takeaway wasn't going to make this feeling go away. Nothing was.

After Mum walked out of the room, Emme felt her whole body heave with another wave of emotion. How could she have let herself believe that just because she and her friends were back together, that Mum and Dad would get back together too?

Emme reached under the cushion and tugged on the programme that had been quickly hidden there. It was crushed and wrinkled, and she tried to flatten it out as the tears started dripping.

She had to make it right again, to convince Mum and Dad to try harder. She had to make it better. The anniversary was just a few days away – and Dad was probably going to start packing any minute.

She had to try.

Chapter 9

Glazed and confused

The bakery was bopping on Sunday. Like on opening day, there was actually a queue out the door.

Daisy had worked out a plan for the special anniversary event. Emme would come and use the kitchen at the bakery over the weekend, and together with Daisy and some of the other bakers, the group would whip up some baked love for Emme's parents. It was Emme's last chance to make the anniversary dinner perfectly enchanted.

Today's baked love came in the form of Nana Belle's old-fashioned lace cookie recipe.

Emme couldn't believe her eyes when Daisy led

her into the back of the bakery. It was like a whole other world back there. Emme could see that this was where the real magic happened.

The square footage in the back of the shop was double the size of the shop itself. It would have to be, of course, since there were machines and stations and supplies stacked everywhere. The room looked like a shiny stainless steel wonderland dusted in snowy icing sugar. Every surface contained a different dessert at a different stage: butter and sugar being creamed, dough being rolled out, cakes being iced. Emme wanted to dip her fingers into everything. She wanted to get busy baking with Daisy!

Towards the back of the bakery there was a wall of beautiful, cavernous ovens. Emme imagined the things that were inside them baking right now. It was the belly of the place, cooking up all kinds of warm, sweet, delicious delights. Daisy Duncan literally made *everything* in her bakery – from scratch, out of thin air, with her hands and heart.

Inside the kitchen, Emme was surprised to see Carlos hard at work with two other baking assistants. She had no idea that many people worked behind the scenes. These workers were like the Oompa Loompas of Daisy's Desserts. Emme could see that they worked very hard to make all the treats come together to brighten people's days and add a little sweetness to their lives.

"How long do you work each day?"

"Do you ever run out of flour?"

"What kinds of fillings are inside these pastry bags?"

Emme asked questions and tasted samples and worked the room with Daisy. It was a world she'd never seen before – and she loved it.

Finally it was time to do the most important task of the day – to make those lace cookies. Daisy took charge to make sure the cookies looked exactly the way Nana Belle's would have. She showed Emme pictures of the miraculous spun sugar – her unique addition to the recipe for a little extra pizzazz. Emme couldn't imagine how they'd be turning plain old sugar into those crystal wisps and ornate lattice shapes.

"How did you become a baker in the first place?" Emme asked as Daisy lined up the ingredients they'd need.

"I went to hotel school," Daisy said. "But mostly I just hung around in the kitchen and tagged along with Nana Belle. The smell of her freshly baked bread gave me power. Don't you feel the power back here?"

Emme chuckled, thinking about that electricity. She nodded. "Definitely!"

"Now," Daisy explained, "lace cookies are named because of the little holes that form when they bake. They are very delicate and you need to be careful that they do not burn when you bake them. Most of baking is science, after all. And paying attention to the details."

Emme was fascinated by the story behind the cookies. The delicate sugar lace could look so perfectly formed, so beautiful, but then it could crack apart with just the smallest amount of pressure. *Kind of like Mum and Dad*, she couldn't help but think.

Daisy explained the origin of this particular recipe. Nana Belle had been kneading dough and baking goodies all of her life. One day, she happened upon a lace cookie recipe, and over the years she fine-tuned it to make her own. The version that Daisy was teaching Emme today was full of family secrets. There were crushed almonds inside and a little bit of cardamom, a spice that Daisy told Emme was very, very precious. There was also a load of butter in the cookies, of course. Butter made everything better.

Emme loved butter on her bagels, but the amount of butter used in the back room of the bakery was truly shocking. Emme counted thirty slabs of it alone in the first mix of ingredients for the lace cookies! Her eyes glazed over at the delicious potential in those creamy dollops.

Daisy rolled the cookies out and laid them onto special pads on the cookie sheets. The pads helped the cookies bake evenly so they would come out perfectly crisp and lightly browned.

Emme watched with delight as ordinary ingredients came together to make something magical. She marvelled at the dance-like routine of the bakers who stirred and rolled and spun and tossed, with Daisy orchestrating it all, calling out instructions and encouragement to her team. Daisy was more than just a fun-loving, frizzy-haired dessert champion. She was a true magician.

The process for making the spun sugar was an entirely separate and wonderful process. Daisy showed Emme how to make it: very carefully.

All that was inside spun sugar was sugar, corn syrup and water. The fun (and hard) part was heating up those ingredients and then playing with them just enough to stretch the sugar into the air as if painting a masterpiece. The sugar was stretched across a small, greased bowl so it would form a shape but not stick to the sides.

Emme was dizzy with all the things there were to consider.

Once the lace cookies had been prepared, Daisy showed Emme how to make teeny spun sugar "hats" for the cookies that gave them a one-of-a-kind look.

"See how it stretches out," Daisy said, showing Emme. "It's like the way a soft caramel stretches when you pull away after a single bite, except that there are many more strands with this."

"I could make – and eat – this all day," Emme said, enraptured with the whole process. They carefully placed each fragile sculpture into a long box that sat open, waiting to be filled.

"My Nana Belle trusted this recipe nearly a century ago," Daisy said. "And I trust it now. I think that one look at these cookies and your Mum and Dad will not be able to stop smiling. How could they not enjoy a dinner that ends with something as enchanting as these?"

Emme was overwhelmed by the different feelings she had going on at the same time. All at once, she burst into tears. There had been a lot of tears these days, and here they were again.

"Emme!" Daisy called out. "What's going on? What's the matter? What happened? Have a seat right now. Talk to me."

Daisy offered Emme a glass of water, then sat in front of her with hands folded, just listening and waiting.

"It doesn't matter," Emme said. "Any of this."

"What do you mean?" Daisy asked.

"They're getting divorced. I can't save them."

Daisy clutched a hand to her heart. Emme's own heart was aching too.

"I know it's hard," Daisy said. "But you can't control what they do, Emme. You can only control yourself. You're here with me, asking for help, because you want to believe. That's powerful stuff."

"Believe in what?"

"Spun sugar, lace cookies, icing, magic, hope.

You told me yourself ..."

Emme sighed. "Yeah. I did. I do."

"You can't make things better unless you believe. Give your mum and dad a special memory. Give them some– "

"BAKED LOVE!" Emme and Daisy said in unison. Emme laughed. It was an odd, but welcome, feeling to switch so quickly from crying to laughing.

Emme wiped away the leftover tears and made a pact with herself that she wouldn't fall apart about this anymore. What would be would be, and she realized she had known that for a long time. But right now, there was work to be done. No matter what, she was going to be the hostess with the mostess for her parents' big night.

Chapter 10

That's how the cinnamon rolls

Emme had managed to coordinate with her parents to make sure that Dad postponed his flight for the business trip on their anniversary. Without giving away too many details, Emme had convinced him that he needed to be at her special dinner on Tuesday *or else.* Dad laughed at the veiled threat, but it worked. Whenever Emme fluttered her "pupy-dog eyes" at him, Dad fell flat.

"*Ohhhh-kay*, Em," he said, defeated. "You win. I will be there on Tuesday. Obviously you've got something up your sleeve. I don't want to be the one to mess it up."

"Good Dad!" Emme chirped.

"Your mother does know this is happening, right?"

Emme nodded. The truth was that Mum *thought* she knew what the whole shindig was about, even though Emme wasn't telling her much about the specifics.

"Look, Emme. I already told you Dad and I are separating," Mum said later with a sigh. "I know it's hard to deal with, but it's only going to be harder if you don't just accept it. I don't want you to meddle."

"Mum!" Emme countered. "You have to let me do this dinner. I promise I won't meddle!"

"I'm sorry," Mum said. "But you need to respect the fact that this is something for your father and me to work through."

"Mum, you don't even know what I'm planning. It's no big deal. Really."

Mum sighed again. "Oh? What are you planning?"

"I'm not telling you! It would ruin the surprise," Emme said. "You always see the half-empty glass, Mum," Emme said. "Just give me a chance."

Mum frowned. "A chance to put us on the spot? Emme, Dad and I ..."

"Please just trust me, Mum," Emme interrupted. "I promise I'm doing this to make you feel good, not bad. Special sugary cookies are a part of my plan."

Mum laughed out loud. "Cookies? Well then, what am I complaining about?" She tilted her head and smiled. "I should have known. You are the sweetest thing in my life," she said, giving Emme a tight hug.

Emme tilted her head. "Oh, Mum."

Mum chuckled. "I know. I better go and plan my big dinner party outfit."

"Yes, you better."

"We'll be there, all dolled up, for you. Only for you, my love. Dad and Mum both."

"Don't forget! You need to stay out of the flat until seven, okay? Same goes for Dad. Got it?"

Mum nodded. "Just remember. I can't make any guarantees about how we will react, Emme. Lately my emotions are all over the place."

"Mine too," Emme confessed.

"It's not too late to postpone your plan."

"MUM! Stop! It will be good. I promise. You will be good too – promise?"

Mum nodded. "For you. Always."

Once her parental special guests were secured, Emme asked Lizzie and Trish to help finish hand-colouring the programmes that they'd created. She mounted all the photographs onto foam core board. She used the backside of last month's science project. Mum would be impressed with her recycling something for a new purpose.

Tuesday afternoon, Lizzie and Trish went shopping with Emme for the special decor. She got streamers in rainbow colours to string up on the ceiling with special tape. She got plastic gold plates and utensils and special fluted glasses for the water. And she got balloons – thirteen half-price balloons with the words "Happy Anniversary!" on them.

She quickly learned that £70 barely added up to streamers, balloons, pasta and some cookies. It was a little over the top, Emme knew, but she didn't care. She needed to make everything count. After all, even though Mum and Dad said they'd made up their mind and the separation was happening, there was a sliver of hope, possibility and the tiniest shard of a chance that they just might reunite. Just *maybe*. Although Trish and Lizzie tried to warn Emme that she might be going overboard and setting herself up for disappointment, Emme stayed the course. She thought of what Daisy said: *believe.* And Emme started to realize that she was doing this as much for herself as for her mum and dad.

When Emme returned home with the balloons and other goodies, including the catered dinner tray, she found herself alone in the apartment. Mum and Dad had listened and kept to their promise to stay away until seven o'clock. She rushed around doing last-minute tasks like setting the table and warming up dinner.

Daisy had wrapped the box of cookies with a giant bow and left them that morning for Seymour the doorman. Emme peeked inside the box to see how the spun sugar, which looked like lace upon lace, had survived since Sunday. No cracks at all. That was a good sign. It was a work of cookie art as far as Emme was concerned. She had never imagined that cookies could be so beautiful.

Especially cookies Emme made!

She carefully displayed the cookies on a large platter so she could bring them out at the end of the meal. The dinner itself was wrapped in foil containers in the oven, so all she had to do was dish it onto plates when they sat down. Dad could pour the wine later. Emme had less than no idea how to use a corkscrew.

At seven on the dot, the doorbell rang once and then three quick times after that, like some sort of secret password. Emme peered through the peephole. Mum and Dad were out there. Standing *together.* Dad had a bouquet of colourful blooms in his arms. Mum was tapping her foot, looking tense. They weren't saying much, but at least they were standing closer than usual. And they were dressed up, as promised.

Emme swung the door open wide. She greeted them in her catering uniform: black T-shirt, black leggings and a black apron that she'd written on in silver marker: HAPPY LUCKY 13TH ANNIVERSARY!

"Welcome!" she cried out. A wayward balloon was sucked out into the corridor, but Dad grabbed it.

"This is certainly festive," Mum said with a wink.

Dad shook his head and patted Emme on the back. "*Festive* isn't the word for it. This is wonderful!"

He handed Emme the bouquet of flowers.

"Oh, Dad," Emme giggled, taking the blooms and inhaling the sweet smell. "Now you both need to sit on the couch while I get everything ready." She handed Mum and Dad each a programme.

Trish and Lizzie had done a great job helping to colour in around Emme's cool lettering. There were stick figures and hearts and little pictures of cookies, a surprise touch.

PRESENTING THE BEST ANNIVERSARY EVER DINNER

Tuesday October 30 at 7 p.m. @ our flat

(don't be early!!!)

MENU

Penne pasta and meatballs from Villarina Trattoria

(Dad's favourite)

Mum's frozen tomato sauce

(defrosted!)

Salad tomatoes & French dressing

Garlic bread

(Mum's favourite)

Special dessert from the new bakery

(and ME!!!!)

ENTERTAINMENT

A walk down "Remmery" (memory) lane with Emme

(whoa – too many rhymes!)

Music from your dating days

CREATED BY YOUR ONE AND ONLY DAUGHTER

I love you, Mum and Dad

Emme!!!

Mum and Dad scanned the programme and read Emme's poem at the bottom. Mum touched her fingers to her lips.

"You did all this?" Dad asked, looking around.

"I can't believe it," Mum said to Dad. "I had no idea, Charlie. Truly."

"Quite the daughter you made, here," Dad said.

"We made," Mum corrected him and touched his elbow.

"Okay! So have an hors d'oeuvre, and then we will get started," Emme said, clicking on the music and handing them a plate of cheese and crackers. Bands called R.E.M. and The Police played through the speakers.

"How old does she think we are?" Dad asked Mum a few minutes later when he heard an Elvis song come on. Emme was bringing out the garlic bread and saw them chuckling together. Emme couldn't remember the last time they had laughed *together* at anything. Was the plan working?

A few crackers and cheese later, Emme set the

steaming pasta on the table and called them to dinner. They made all kinds of enthusiastic comments about the meal, but neither Mum nor Dad talked much with each other. At least they were peacefully eating the food. That was something.

"Aren't you going to eat?" Mum asked Emme halfway through the meal.

"Not now," Emme said. "I'm working here."

"Ha!" Dad laughed. "I could get used to this!"

"You certainly are working very hard," Mum said. "We'll just stay put then until you give us further instructions."

With Emme running back and forth to the kitchen, Mum and Dad were forced to interact. They politely chatted about work and the latest news headlines. There had been a huge accident on the motorway that day. They made conversation about that – about anything except each other. But at least they were talking.

When dinner was officially finished, Emme cleared the table.

"I have an announcement now," Emme said. "Before I bring out the big surprise, I just want to say that this is your thirteenth anniversary and I know – I understand – that this will possibly be your last as a couple. But I want to make this thirteenth celebration lucky, not unlucky. Because I am always hopeful." She pulled out the cookie tray and proudly held it out to her parents.

"Extraordinary!" Dad said when he saw the platter. "How did you ...?"

But Mum dropped her head.

"Mum? Are you okay?" Emme asked.

She had to excuse herself and leave the table. She wasn't crying. She almost looked mad.

"Oh, dear," Dad said. He sat back in his chair. "I'm sorry, Emme. This is a hard time for your mother and me." He swiped at his wet eyes. Maybe this whole plan had been too emotional.

"Dad," Emme said softly, sitting down in Mum's chair, whispering now. "It's hard for me too, you know?"

"Emme, I'm so sorry," Dad said and took a deep breath. "I know you meant well, Emme, but this dinner, this anniversary, it's not going to change anything. Your mother and I have made up our minds, honey. We know this is for the best. I know, *I know,* this is hard."

"You have no idea how hard, Dad. You're never even here to see how hard it is!"

"Emme!" he called, but she jumped up and went to find Mum in the bathroom. She was washing her face and taking a cold drink of water.

"I'm so sorry, Mum," Emme said. "You were right. This was a bad idea. My idea was so lame. Dad's still leaving."

Mum turned to Emme and planted a soft kiss on her forehead. "My dear Emme," Mum said. "I am so sorry. I am sorry that we have not been able to fix this between your father and me. This was a decision we both made – not just Dad. I'm sorry we haven't been paying better attention to your needs."

Emme felt her whole body shake.

Mum quickly kissed away a single teardrop. "No crying. No yelling. And no running away. Let's go and have one of those gorgeous lace cookies. Let's go and talk and be a family. For tonight."

"How?"

"We will make this anniversary matter. We will make it lucky. Like you said. Come on. Dad is waiting. I'm ready."

When they walked back out, Dad had his sleeves rolled all the way up. He was starting to wash dishes and clean up the entire dinner mess.

"Dad!" Emme cried out. "Leave that. I'm cleaning up. Not you."

Mum went over to Dad. "Thanks, Charlie," she said quietly. "For showing up."

Dad threw his arms around Mum. "I'm sorry for not being here."

A part of Emme wished that all those sorry words meant they'd stay together forever and ever. But she knew it was just for now. Just for this minute.

And that was okay.

Emme wrapped her arms around both parents.

Her heart was thumping so hard.

The three of them sat around the table and devoured the magical lace cookies, right down to the last twirl of spun sugar. It was like eating happiness, Mum said. She hadn't smiled this much in weeks, maybe months. Neither had Dad. And neither had Emme.

The next morning on the way to school, Emme walked by Daisy's Desserts. Daisy was right up front putting a tray of apple bars into one of the cases.

"So?" Daisy said when she spied Emme walking into the bakery.

"So …" Emme said, half-smiling.

"Did Nana Belle's lace cookies work?" Daisy asked with raised eyebrows. "Did they do their magic in honour of the lucky thirteenth anniversary?"

Emme shrugged. "Not really. Well, sort of. I suppose so. Yes. They did."

"That doesn't sound so decisive. What happened?"

Emme explained about the programme and the dinner. She told Daisy how she'd even put on a dress and made up some comical interpretive dance moves to one of Mum's favourite songs to end the evening on a humorous note.

Daisy laughed. "Didn't know dance was on your menu," she said. "You really went *all* out."

"I wasn't going to at first," Emme said. "But I wanted to do anything and everything possible to make them happy, even if just for Tuesday night."

"And?"

"They're still splitting up," Emme said, resigned.

"Ahhh," Daisy said. "So the cookie power didn't work?"

"No, it did," Emme said with a small smile.

Everything Emme had talked about with Daisy before the anniversary surprise had mattered.

"The recipe worked," Emme went on. "Mum and Dad thought this was the nicest night they'd had together in years. That's what they said. The cookies were the most magical part. We talked about how even though they're splitting, *we're* not. I feel more like a family than I've felt for a long time. Mum and Dad both said they'll pay more attention to all the in-between stuff. We will still be a family, just different. With less fighting and more sugar."

"I'm so glad to hear that," Daisy said. "I'm glad that you shared your story with me and that the bakery could help you out."

"Mum and Dad may be separating, but I was thinking, maybe now I can get *more* cookies," Emme smiled mischievously. "We can stock up on Daisy's Desserts at two locations – Mum's and Dad's!"

Just then, more of the morning crowd rushed inside the bakery in a long queue for their croissants and doughnuts and coffee.

"I have to skedaddle," Daisy said, flipping some loose curls out of her eyes. She was wearing a perfect flowered dress this morning with striped woolly socks and Birkenstocks on her feet. Daisy even had little daisies painted on her fingernails.

"Thank you so much," Emme said. "I hope I can come back and bake with you again one day."

"Hmm," Daisy said. "That gives me a good idea. We'll talk soon!" She disappeared behind the counter. "New queue forms over here!" she bellowed.

Emme whisked out of the shop and started to walk to school. She knew she'd be late, but she decided it was worth it.

Daisy had made all the difference for her last night. Nothing could take away that magical feeling of joy and accomplishment, even if the end result wasn't quite what Emme hoped it would be.

Emme and her lace cookies had reminded Mum and Dad about what mattered again. And then there was that family hug.

Sometimes love is beautiful and fragile. And sometimes it's strong. Emme knew that no matter what happened, those strings that tied the three of them together would never break.

Back to the blog

Home
Meet the bakers
Recipes
- Cakes
- Cookies
- Tray bakes
- Breads
- Gluten free
- Vegan
- Dairy free
- Other

Archive
- January
- February
- March

Dear Sweeties,

Sometimes baking has rewards beyond the caramel brownie dusted with sugar. My Nana Belle used to always say, "It's not whether you win or lose, it's how you bake the cake."

I agree with her one-hundred per cent!

Thank you, friends and neighbours, for welcoming Daisy's Desserts into this neighbourhood. It's only been a few weeks, but this already feels like home, thanks to your warm welcome!

I think some of the best treats for me have come via tweenagers who continue to camp out at the tables here and do their homework! I love you all!

And for my very dear friend with the lace cookies: Life has a funny way of working itself out. Stay strong!

Head's up, everyone! Daisy's Desserts will soon be launching some cool cooking classes right here in the shop. It's a perfect way to meet new friends and add something sweet to your life.

See you in the kitchen!

xo, Daisy

Emme's lace cookies

Baking is a blast when you make special treats for your family and friends. With this easy recipe, you can make cookies like Emme did in the story. Just make sure you ask an adult for help with the oven or hob when you bake. Daisy would want you to be extra careful in the kitchen!

Ingredients:

50 grams brown sugar
55 grams butter (½ stick)
3 tablespoons corn syrup
30 grams plain flour
Baking parchment
Cookie sheet

Directions:

1. Mix the sugar, butter and corn syrup in a saucepan on low heat.

2. Stir until it melts.

3. Slowly stir in the flour until the mixture is smooth.

4. Place baking parchment on a cookie sheet.

5. Drop the batter onto the cookie sheet in small spoonfuls, about 2.5 centimetres apart.

6. Bake for 5 minutes at 190 degrees Celsius.

7. When cookies are ready they will be bubbly and brown. Cool on a rack.

Bonus: Adding spun sugar to the top of the cookies might be complicated for beginning bakers, but here's a fun trick: Shape the cookies into rolls or funnels when they are still warm, and they'll cool into the shape you wish!

Meet the bakers

Daisy

Owner of Daisy's Desserts! With a frizzy head of magical red hair, sunny disposition and a treasure trove of recipes passed down from her dear Nana Belle, this always-optimistic baker is ready to serve you! Along with her crazy baking team — Dina, Babs and Carlos — Daisy aims to transform our city neighbourhood with sugar, spice and everything nice. From custard tarts to cupcakes, Daisy always seems to have the recipe for "baked love" up her flour-dusted sleeve. Inside Daisy's Desserts, the impossible somehow becomes iced with possibility!

Dina

Baker and waitress Dina specializes in sweets, especially when it comes to her personality! Designated mother hen of the crew, Dina not only has a way with a rolling pin and a whisk but also with our customers! She is always suggesting new recipes and encouraging Daisy to try new ingredients from around the globe.

Carlos

Daisy's number-one confidante and trusted sidekick in the kitchen, Carlos has a twinkle in his eye and pep in his step. A family man with four sweet-toothed children at home, Carlos is always inventing and testing new recipes in the kitchen of Daisy's Desserts. He is the master mix-man — to date, he's invented cookies, cakes and even Daisy's line of sweet treats for dogs. His favourite saying is, "I keep experimenting until I find the right formula!"

Babs

Like a Hollywood starlet from another era, Babs is always dressed to impress with a bouffant do and an apron to match every shade of lipstick. Our wisecracking baking beauty has a lingo all her own, calling customers "peach" or "sugar" before sneaking them samples of Daisy's latest baked goodies. Babs is also our bakery's guardian angel — years ago, she was BFFs with Daisy's Nana Belle.

Talk it out with Daisy!

Everyone faces tough times – Emme knows this all too well. But good friends can help!

Can you think of a challenging time in your life that friends helped you through?

What made you feel better?

What made you feel worse?

Was there a time you were there for a friend to lean on when she needed support?

Good friends can help you through life's challenges. Come up with some examples in the story where you see evidence of good friendships.

Laura Dower

About the author

Laura Dower worked in marketing and editorial in children's publishing for many years before taking a big leap to the job of full-time author. She has published more than 100 children's books, including the popular tween series *From the Files of Madison Finn*. A longtime Girl Scout leader and Cub Scout leader, Laura lives with her family in New York, USA.

Lilly Lazuli

About the illustrator

London based illustrator Lilly Lazuli has a penchant for all things colourful and sweet! Originally from Hawaii, Lilly creates artwork that has a bright and cheerful aesthetic. She gains most of her inspiration from travelling, vintage fashion and ogling beautiful cakes. She enjoys making eye-catching artwork that makes people smile.

For MORE GREAT BOOKS go to

www.raintree.co.uk